Cynthia Blake has a problem. She was sure dating twelve men in one year, then marrying one at the end was a great way to find a husband, but with three suitors down and nine to go, her little experiment has gotten out of hand.

Someone clearly has it out for her and is doing their best to trash her reputation, threatening to take down her beloved chain of ice cream stores in the process. And even though she's having fun (a *lot* of fun) with each of her Flavors of the Month, choosing one is going to be harder than she ever imagined.

In this sequel to *The Plan*, follow Cynthia through April, May, and June as things heat up just in time for summer. Can she get things back on track before her dream of love melts away??

THE

PREDICAMENT

Flavors of the Month, Book Two

Penny McLean

A NineStar Press Publication
www.ninestarpress.com

The Predicament

First Edition, January 2024

ISBN: 978-1-64890-729-6

Also available in eBook, ISBN: 978-1-64890-728-9

CONTENT WARNING:
This book contains sexually explicit content, which may only be suitable for mature readers. Depictions of multiple partners, cheating, and shaming.

To Nicci: For your unwavering support, friendship, and honesty. These books could never have been completed without you. Thank you for helping me get to the finish line, literary and otherwise.

Chapter One

March 28

It's weird to be in such a familiar place with a complete stranger. I know every twist and turn of Disneyland, but when I look at the guy walking next to me, I keep realizing again what a strange path I've been on this year.

"So, you dated Peter as part of your Plan?" Eric asks, as I finish explaining everything that's happened since I set this all in to motion in December.

I nod. "But we met back in high school. I had a huge crush on him back in the day and he thought he had one on me."

"But he really liked that Cara girl?"

"Apparently," I say sheepishly. "People used to confuse us from time to time, but this has to be the worst instance of mistaken identity I've ever experienced."

"I'll say. I once had a girl throw eggs at my door back in London. When I yelled down to ask what she was doing, she said she meant to hit my neighbor's house, but got the number wrong. That was annoying. Yours is worse."

I laugh really hard and smile at Eric as we stroll down Main Street toward Sleeping Beauty's Castle. It's crowded today and we've already had to dodge a few strollers pushed by frantic parents, eager to maximize their children's happiness for the day. It looks exhausting.

We stop for a minute to sit on a bench and watch the people passing by. Or rather, Eric is watching the other people, while I'm taking the opportunity to stare at him and assess his looks. It's shallow, but I don't care.

The verdict? He is really, really cute. The glasses I noticed the first time I saw him currently sit askew on his face, or they do until he reaches up to adjust them. His black hair is unkempt, most likely because we drove all night to get here. His eyes are a steely gray and his build is tall and lanky.

"Why did you bring me here?" I say as the thought occurs to me. "Don't get me wrong; I'm thrilled. But what put it in your head to get in the car and drive straight here?"

"Well, I haven't lived in America very long, but I did a lot of touristy things pretty early. I came here last year with a coworker while we were visiting a lab in Los Angeles, and I thought how nice it would be to come back with a woman on a date. So, when I saw you looking like you needed an escape last night, I decided this would be the best option."

"And you went to the Prom last night just to see me?" I'm still a bit mystified.

"Indeed, I did. Something about seeing your legs dangle outside of my tree that night really left an impression."

We're both laughing again, but I'm secretly wondering if he's holding back regarding our second encounter. I decide not to mention it and opt for the best distraction I can think of.

"How about I buy you a churro and we go check out a ride?"

"Buy me a what?" he says.

"You didn't have a churro when you came here before?" I'm shocked that he missed something so crucially Disney. He shakes his head, so I grab his hand to lead us to the nearest cart, just opening for the day.

"Allow me to introduce you to the greatest thing since sliced bread." I pay for two churros and hand one to him. They are warm and smell amazing. I smile as he takes a bite of his and wait to bite into my own cinnamon-sugar treat until I hear his assessment.

"Oh wow," he says. "I had no idea what I was missing out on."

I laugh and lead us into Fantasyland to get in line for Peter Pan. As we queue up, Eric smiles. "Don't hate me, but I didn't ride this ride either. Guessing it's a favorite of yours since you brought me here first?"

"Oh yes." I nod and smile. "I really do love this ride, but it also gets a long line pretty early, so it's best to come here before it gets too bad."

"You're quite the expert." He seems impressed.

"You could say that. So, how did you end up in the States?"

We pass the time in line with Eric filling me in on the work he does as a physicist. It's all really complicated, and I understand very little, but he's patient with me and explains as best he can. He came to America with another Brit named Allen and they're both working on some big breakthrough with a professor at Arizona State University.

"That's really cool," I say as we board the flying pirate ship that will take us around on the ride. Eric holds my hand as the lap bar comes down and it's such a sweet gesture that I well up a bit. This ride does that to me anyway, but maybe I'm already feeling a nice connection with this new guy. Either way, it's a great start to the day. And month. And maybe my happily ever after.

Chapter Two

www.flavorsofthemonth.bloggerific.com

No joke, friends—April is here and we're already one-fourth of the way through my crazy dating experiment. I am excited to announce that I found a guy for this month the old-fashioned way: by accidentally hitting him in the head with my shoe. Just kidding. Long story. But really, I met him in person and things are already going great. Come on down to any Sinfully Good location this month to try Royal Cinnamon Swirl. It's basically churro ice cream. You're welcome.

I have both May and June candidates lined up for myself, so keep that in mind if you're sending me an email any time soon. Summer is wide open though, and I hope to hear from you soon!

April 2

E ric and I had a perfect day at Disneyland, and an even better night at the hotel. After taking a tour of Fantasyland, I walked him around to the other areas of the park, pointing out little things as we went.

"And that's the spot where I tripped when I was five years old and got this scar," I say, pointing out a line on my knee my Dad always called "the only free souvenir we ever got at Disneyland." We're in line for the Matterhorn and I remember running up the path before hitting the pavement, hard.

"Poor baby," he says, kissing my hand he's currently holding.

"It was no big deal. I cried until a Cast Member brought me a balloon and a Band-Aid."

"I know, I was just looking for an excuse to kiss you." He looks down at the ground.

"Oh." I blush. It would be the perfect moment to lean up and kiss him back, but we're shoved from behind by an impatient teenager who is annoyed that we're holding up the line.

We both shrug and keep walking until it's our turn to ride. We laugh our way down the mountain on the bumpy bobsleds and I can't help but smile as we exit together, while Eric holds the little gate open for me.

I show him all my favorite places in the park, and he continues to tell me about his work, life back home in London, and anything else we can think of. The conversation never lags and I'm not sure if it's because we're both surrounded by so much joy or if there's an actual spark happening here. But I really don't care.

Normally, I'm all in favor of spending the entire day at Disneyland, but by midday, we're both getting exhausted. I'm really dragging and can only imagine how Eric feels, having driven us there.

"Should we find a hotel?" I ask, mid-yawn. I'm very aware of the implications of that question as Eric begins to blush.

"I'd like that," he says, his yawn now mirroring mine. "I was thinking I could maybe drive us back home tonight, but I'm not sure that would be safe."

I get on the phone and call to see if there are any rooms available at the on-site hotels. Eric got the tickets, so I tell him I'll cover the hotel, but he insists and grabs the phone from me. He steps away so I can't hear.

"How does a room at the Grand Californian sound?" he asks, coming back victorious.

"Heavenly," I say. It's just a short walk and I'm pretty sure I could take the greatest nap of all time. We're still holding hands as we walk back up Main Street toward the park gates and Eric comes to a stop, so I do the same.

I look around to see what made him put on the brakes, but he's just nodding.

"This is it," he says.

"This is what?"

"This is where we should have our first kiss." He pulls me to him.

And we do. Surrounded by people walking in either direction who now have to detour around us, Eric and I kiss. It's a slow, searching kiss at first, tentative in the best way. We're still getting to know each other, but it's hard not to feel romantic in this place, especially for two sleep-deprived people running on nothing but churros. We kiss for a semi-inappropriate amount of time, especially considering the number of children who can see us, but it's such a lovely moment that neither of us can be bothered to worry about anything but each other.

"Well done, you," he says, pleased with my performance.

"Back at ya," I say, leading him the rest of the way out of the park.

We walk the short distance to the entrance of the Grand Californian and check in to our room. The lobby is as beautiful as I remember it, full of comfy-looking chairs and couches and decked out with dark wood everywhere. There's a piano player softly scoring the moment with "So This is Love" from Cinderella and I am soon humming along.

As we walk up to our hotel room, I am struck by the notion that I'm about to spend the night with a guy I barely know. Getting in the car with him was crazy enough, but suddenly the intimacy of a hotel room feels like a really big deal.

"I really like you," he says, opening the door for me and holding it. "And I'd be lying if I said I'm not attracted to you, but we can just sleep in here if you like. Or, you know, maybe kiss a bit too, or something, but we don't have to do anything more than that."

I smile and nod, reassured by his statement. I look at the bed and see both an opportunity to get even more intimate with this guy, or, more importantly, to catch up on some sleep.

"For now," I say, taking off my shirt and jeans, "how about we take a nap in our underwear? Best of both worlds?"

He laughs, but also begins to undress.

"I must be exhausted if I can resist you looking like that," he says, walking toward me as I pull back the covers. "But yeah, I think that's a great idea."

We climb in bed together and quickly ease ourselves into a big spoon/little spoon situation. I'm wrapped up in Eric's arms and feeling delirious when I hear his breathing slow and realize he's already asleep. Before I can even begin to marvel about how quickly he did that, I'm out as well.

*

I'm not sure how long we sleep, but when I wake up, it's pitch-black in our room and I'm feeling much better. I unwind myself from Eric's arms and walk to the window to look out on our view. We're facing Disneyland and I smile as I look out over the tops of some of my favorite places in the world.

I hear Eric stir behind me and look back to see him smiling up at me.

"That's a beautiful view," he says.

"I know, right? I think we'll be able to see the fireworks when they start."

"I meant the nearly naked woman standing at the window." He raises his eyebrows at me.

"Ah." I'm lucky that it's dark so he can't see me blush. I don't feel especially beautiful at this moment, standing in a mismatched cotton bra and underwear, still also wearing the ankle socks I forgot to kick off before our nap. Before I can get too down on myself, Eric stands up to join me.

His glasses are sitting on the bedside table, so I take the opportunity to look deeply into his eyes. They're looking right back into mine and it's an intense moment until he says, "You're a bit blurry. Mind if I grab my specs?"

I laugh and go up on my tiptoes to kiss him. I realize he must have been leaning over to kiss me before and smile as he stoops a bit once again to kiss me back. It's dark and we're now pressed up against each other in nothing but our underwear. I know where this is going.

Eric brings his hands up to my face, then into my hair as our kiss deepens. He seems to have forgotten about his glasses for the moment and I wonder just how blind he is as he leaves my lips and begins to kiss my neck. I nearly giggle as he moves to the other side of my neck, kissing a ticklish spot on my collarbone as he goes. He slides my bra strap down and finds my shoulder as his next conquest.

We both jump as the first of the Disneyland fireworks explodes across the sky.

"Stop me if I'm going too fast," he says, earnestly, "but how many guys can say they've made you see fireworks when you've kissed?"

"A couple," I admit. "But I don't think anyone can say they've made me see fireworks while we've fucked."

"Oh my. Guess I'll just have to be the first."

I laugh and throw my head back as Eric turns me a bit so I'm facing the window. He's behind me now and kissing my back while reaching around to feel my breasts, still sitting in my comfy T-shirt bra. Eric moves up to kiss the back of my neck while unfastening the clasp and slowly slides the straps down and off until I am topless against the glass.

"If anyone has binoculars and impeccable timing, they've got one hell of a view right now," he says. "Or so I assume."

The whole thing is simultaneously so hot and romantic that I can hardly stand it. I'm still watching the fireworks go off throughout the sky as Eric pulls down my panties and helps me step out of them. I hear him shimmy out of his underwear and soon he's pressed up behind me, naked and clearly as into this as I am.

"I'd normally take my time," he says, reaching down with his hands to spread my legs apart. "But as I don't know how long the fireworks will last..."

He doesn't finish that sentence and instead enters me from behind. He's guiding me up and down onto him with his hands on my hips and I gasp as I take him in fully. Maybe it's because I'm coming out of a relationship with a guy with a tiny dick, or maybe Eric is just well-endowed, but he feels especially large, long, and perfect to me at the moment. So long, in fact, that I bump my knee against the wall during one especially enthusiastic thrust.

We start out slowly and Eric moves his hands to my tits, now blocking them from any Disney peeping Toms who may have been in the area. I lean my head back and Eric reaches down to kiss my cheek as he glides in and out of me. We reach our finale at the same time the fireworks do, then collapse in a heap back onto the bed.

As I look at the bruise on my leg from our firework-sex, I laugh as I realize it's the second free souvenir I've gotten from Disneyland.

*

"**H**e could have been a murderer," says Meg, once again trying to retroactively talk me out of taking a spontaneous road trip with a complete stranger. "Do you have any idea how worried we were?"

"Tell Fred I'm sorry for putting you both through that," I say earnestly. "I really didn't mean to make you worry."

"Not Fred. I mean, he was worried too. I meant Kim. She went after you at the Prom and saw you leave with him. She was terrified that you were making a terrible decision because you were mad at her."

"I was mad at her. I'm still mad at her. Are they together?"

"Not getting in the middle of this." Meg holds up both hands as if to indicate I'm on my own.

"Fine. But really, do you forgive me for my dangerous decision-making? And do you want to hear how the trip went?"

She smiles and I know I've chosen the right way to distract her. I tell her all about my day and night at Disneyland and even give her a few of the steamy details from my magical sex romp, as I am now referring to it.

"He's what would happen if a Disney Prince came to life and was really good in bed," I say, smiling at my analogy. "It's what you always hope went down for those Princesses once the credits rolled."

She laughs at this and slaps the table, clearly making some sort of realization in her head. "His name is Eric!" she exclaims.

"Yes." I'm glad to see she's been paying attention.

"Prince Eric!" she says, and I immediately catch her drift.

"*The Little Mermaid*," we both say together.

Now, maybe not all girls fantasized about Disney Princes, but if you happened to be just the right age when *The Little Mermaid* came out, there are good odds he was your first crush. At least, he was for us. With that black hair and sexy smile, it was hard not to fall for him, animated or not. Meg, Kim, and I used to fight over who would get to marry him someday. You know, assuming he came to life and we met him or something.

"You could marry Prince Eric," she says in a reverent whisper.

"I could," I say, not caring at all how massively premature this is. "I really could."

We're both still smiling at this revelation when our waitress brings the two glasses of wine we ordered. I'm about to lift mine to my lips for a first sip when Meg slides hers over in front of me and smiles.

"Not thirsty?" I ask, confused by the gesture.

"Oh, I am," she says. "But people get super judgy when pregnant women drink, so I thought I'd let you take one for the team."

I jump up to hug her, jostling the table and spilling both glasses as we scream and cry together.

"You're pregnant!" I'm dumbfounded as we pull apart so I can sit back down.

"A bona fide honeymoon baby," she confirms. "I feel like absolute shit, but we're so excited."

"Aww—I hate that you feel bad. But this is the best news ever. I'm so, so happy for you."

I'm even happier for her once I've finished both glasses of wine. After I put my hand on her belly for the third time, assuring her I can definitely feel the baby kick, she reminds me that Baby is the size of a pea and puts me in a car to take me home.

I can't stop smiling the whole way there. A new baby for Meg and Prince Eric for me. What a wonderful world.

Chapter Three

April 5

And a wonderful world it continues to be as Eric and I curl up on my couch to watch a movie. We haven't seen each other since coming home from our Disneyland trip, but I feel completely at ease with him again already. I was worried that everything would feel different once the magic faded, but we're zip-ah-dee-doing just fine. Yeah, I went there.

We decided to watch *Enchanted* because Eric mentioned he'd never seen it after I referenced it on our trip. By referenced it, I of course mean I casually broke into one of the songs from the movie, but you get the drill. I like a man who can watch a Disney musical with me without getting sarcastic or snide. He doesn't even seem to mind that I sing along a bit as we watch.

I can't help but wonder if I'm in a similar situation as Giselle finds herself. No girl could be sad to end up with a prince like James Marsden (yum), but who could resist the equally yummy Patrick Dempsey character? I don't think there is a wrong answer for her, but maybe there is a slightly more correct answer. Is that true for me too? And if so, who is Eric in this situation? Is Carter the only other contender at the moment? I thought Javier was still on the same page as me, but he might be in someone else's book now.

That thought makes my heart ache for a moment and I quickly remind myself to come back to the present. Giselle is singing around Central Park about how to know if a guy really loves you and I catch Eric tapping his finger to the rhythm as he holds my hand. I smile as the song goes on and try to quell the rising feeling inside me that I'm falling for this guy a little too hard and a little too fast.

"Want some ice cream?" I say, getting up to go fix us each a bowl before even waiting for him to reply.

"I thought you'd never ask," he says. "I hate to confess this, but I'm actually just dating you for the frozen treats."

"I knew it," I laugh. "Always the ice cream maker, never the bride."

I can't tell if there's a bit of hesitancy in his laugh now that I've hinted at marriage during our second date. I make myself busy in the kitchen while he continues to watch the movie, then hand him a bowl so we can eat and watch at the same time.

"Mmm, this is delicious," he says, approvingly. "What is it?"

"It's your flavor." I'm happy to hear he likes it. "I made it with you in mind. Do you taste the churro inspiration?"

"I do." He takes another bite. "I had no idea I was this delicious."

We meet eyes as he makes this remark, and my mind immediately goes straight down a naughty path at the implication that he might taste just as good. It looks like Eric is on the same train of thought as he's now looking at me a bit more intensely than before.

We both set our bowls on the coffee table and kiss each other quickly. I can taste hints of the ice cream on his lips and it's sweet and sexy at the same time.

"I have an idea," he says, leaning forward to pick up his bowl. He pulls his spoon out of the bowl and dribbles some of the ice cream onto my neck. It's already a bit melted, so it slides from there down my chest and into my cleavage.

Pleased with himself at this result, Eric begins to lick the ice cream off my skin until his face is buried between my breasts. He pauses for just long enough to pull my shirt off over my head, then grabs the bowl and drizzles more ice cream, this time more focused on the area that will soon make my bra a sticky mess.

He licks it off again, tantalizingly slow at first, teasing in his move-ments as he pulls down each cup to take first my left then my right breast into his mouth. I reach back to pull off my bra and Eric gives a delighted sigh.

"I couldn't see you all that well in the dark and without my glasses before," he says, admiringly. "You're so damn sexy."

"You're not so bad yourself," I say, pulling his shirt off over his head as well. In the better light, I can see him fully this time, and I smile at his pale chest, which I assume is the calling card of British men. He has spent most of his college life and career in labs, leaving little time for the gym, but he is strong enough and looks just fine to me.

He pulls me close, and I can feel the stickiness of my chest up against him as we kiss again. We're still pressed together as Eric leans me back down onto the couch so I'm now lying with him on top of me. He kisses his way down my chest and stomach and stops to pull off my pants and underwear. He grabs the ice cream again and makes a trail of ice cream from my belly button down between my thighs and goose bumps form on my skin in anticipation of what's to come.

He licks every drop of ice cream up again, but then reaches back to grab more. Methodically, he pools the next batch in and around my private parts and enthusiastically starts licking it off. I now know how they should teach young men to please a woman and it absolutely involves licking ice cream off her clitoris. In an effort to be thorough, Eric is hitting all the right places and making me feel like I could scream. His tongue is strong and active and after a few minutes and a couple more drops of ice cream from the bowl, I arch my back and let the sweet rush of this orgasm flood through my body.

Before I can sit up and offer to return the favor, Eric has stood up and removed his clothes. He sits back down on the couch, offers me a hand up, then brings me down to sit on his lap, so that we're both facing the TV. I'll admit it—this is the first time I've had sex while watching a Disney movie, but it's surprisingly sexy. Eric has one hand on my hips, keeping us together as he thrusts me up and down in a bouncing motion, and the other hand holds my breast as he squeezes and pinches my erect nipples with just the right amount of pleasure and pain.

We finish at the same time the movie does and I laugh when I realize our climax comes right as the credits roll to the song "Ever Ever After."

"Whoops," he says, looking at the screen. "Guess I'll have to watch it again to see how she decides which guy to end up with."

You and me both.

Chapter Four

April 7

E verything is going great with Eric, and even though I have both May and June already set, I decide to sit down and sift through the emails that have been piling up. There are some great contenders and it's not long before I'm starting to think I could really have an amazing summer.

As I read about these different men though, the thought of moving on from Eric hits me in a way I would never have expected this early on. It was hard to move forward after Carter and even harder after Javier, but I'm not sure how or why I should keep going. I'm scrolling through the emails absentmindedly as I contemplate this predicament when one subject line jumps out at me.

Pictures of you with J, K and P, it reads.

I noticed one earlier that just said *Pictures,* but I assumed it was spam. But realizing those three letters likely stand for Javier, Ken, and Peter, I hold my breath and click to open it.

> *Venmo $10,000 immediately to @GossipAZ or I'll release*
>
> *the pictures I've collected so far of you and your boyfriends.*
>
> *And trust me—you don't want these to go public.*

What the fuck? How could someone have taken pictures of us without me noticing? This has to be a joke. But something about that Venmo handle gives me pause. There's a trashy website called *Gossip A to Z* that routinely posts tabloid-style takedowns of locals. I've never given it much thought, other than to roll my eyes and try to forget it exists, but now I'm recalling a few business owners, athletes, and politicians who have had some pretty embarrassing stuff posted about them. Some posts were even career-ending.

Why would that site be targeting me?

I click reply and try to compose a calm response, but I am not calm and no response comes to mind. I know my little experiment has caught the attention of some local and national websites already, so I don't doubt there's an interest in any pictures that might have been taken, but they can't have anything too juicy or they'd have bypassed the bribery route and gone straight for posting them.

I'm furious and confused and in no way equipped to handle this right now. Some crises are best faced head-on, but my first instinct is to ignore this and run away for the moment. Which is exactly what I'm thinking when I call Eric and invite him to meet me for dinner.

We meet at a little Italian place near my house, and I waste no time filling him in on the disturbing email situation.

"The email didn't mention you," I say, showing him my phone. "But if someone does have pictures of the other three guys I've dated this year, I'd assume they could be trying to get some of us as well."

"I see," he says, considering. "I'm not terribly worried about being associated with a bright, beautiful woman publicly, but I'm not crazy about the whole threat thing. Are you okay?"

"I'm about two glasses of wine short of okay. It's a creepy feeling to know I've been watched these last few months, but even worse to think I haven't noticed it at all. I almost want them to post what they have just so I can see when and where they were able to get photographs of me without my knowledge."

As I'm saying that, an icy feeling goes down my back as I scan the restaurant for someone sitting in a trench coat with a lens pointing at Eric and me. It's a ridiculous idea, but I've seen too many movies to shake the image.

"What's the worst thing they could have pictures of?" Eric asks, taking my hand. "Anything to be really worried about?"

I consider this for a moment. Other than publicly outing the men I've been dating, the pictures really can't be that bad. I definitely need to warn Javier, Ken, and Peter so they aren't blindsided if/when the pictures are published, but I assume they contain nothing more than us holding hands or maybe kissing in public. I'm openly dating them though, so is that really a bad thing?

"I guess not. It's not like we've been out robbing banks or anything. But before I forget, I should give them all a heads-up that something might be coming.

"Of course." Eric gives me my hand back so I can fire off a quick text. I keep it brief and to the point, then put my phone back away to focus on the man sitting across from me.

"So," I begin, excitedly. "Now that that's behind us, I wanted to ask you some questions."

"What kind of questions?"

"Just some basic getting-to-know-you questions. I've kinda been asking each guy this year the same series of questions to see how compatible we are."

"Hit me," he says. "I'm an open book."

1. Given the choice of anyone in the world, who would you want as a dinner guest? (Eric's British roots are on display right off the bat when he says, "Queen Elizabeth," without a moment's hesitation. "I just think she would be so interesting to talk to," he continues. "And I feel like I could talk her into making me a knight. I'm not sure why, but maybe after a few glasses of wine she'd just be like, 'Oh fine, kneel.'")

2. Would you like to be famous? In what way? (This is a bit awkward, considering dating me may now potentially include a bit of local fame. Especially when Eric says he can't think of any circumstances

that would make him want to be famous. "British tabloids are the worst," he adds. "The thought of being around any part of that world makes me queasy." Again, awkward, considering he may be facing that with me, but here's hoping we keep it under control.)

3. Before making a telephone call, do you ever rehearse what you are going to say? Why? ("I've never thought about it," he says, "but I suppose I do. Now that I'm so far away from my family, we have to rely so much more on the phone to stay in touch and I at least prep for each conversation before we start. Not sure why, but I must do it subconsciously.")

4. What would constitute a "perfect" day for you? (Eric makes me blush with his answer, looking into my eyes and saying, "I'd say our day and evening at Disneyland was pretty perfect." I smile and agree. But it's what he says about why it was perfect that makes my heart soar. "It's not like I need some big event or destination to make the day perfect," he explains. "But seeing you so happy as you showed me around was really lovely. I could see it through your eyes, and it was just magical.")

5. When did you last sing to yourself? To someone else? (We both laugh as we recall singing "It's a Small World" on that eponymous ride. He admits that's the first time he's sung in front of anyone in a long time, but says it was so fun and he'd definitely be open to singing with me again.)

6. If you were able to live to the age of ninety and retain either the

mind or body of a thirty-year-old for the last sixty years of your life, which would you want? (In the fastest answer to this question ever, my scientist guy says he'd definitely choose his mind. So much of his life revolves around thinking through life's great mysteries he can't imagine a world where he is unable to do that.)

7. Do you have a secret hunch about how you will die? (On the opposite end of the spectrum, Eric takes his time pondering this one. He's lost friends and family through the years to various things and ultimately decides the best deaths are the ones you have time to prepare for. "As awful as it was to see my granddad die of cancer," he says, thoughtfully, "he had time to get his affairs in order and make sure he told everyone just what we meant to him. I'd like to have that same chance.")

8. Name three things you and your partner appear to have in common. (Eric looks at me for about thirty seconds before admitting he's not quite sure yet. "I know we're compatible," he says, "and I love spending time with you. But as for what we have in common? I'm excited to learn.")

9. For what in your life do you feel most grateful? ("The opportunities I've had," he says. "Being able to come to a new country and do work that is meaningful to me is hugely important. Not everyone can say that. I would hate to work at a job just for the sake of paying bills. Here, I get to contribute and that fulfills me.")

10. If you could change anything about the way you were raised,

what would it be? ("I wish I'd been a bit more confident as a kid," he confesses. "I'm not quite sure how my parents could have instilled that in me, but I was so shy it was painful at times. Maybe if I'd seen my dad be more assertive, it would have helped? But he's so great and that's not fair. I guess I'm not sure on this one.")

11. Take four minutes and tell your partner your life story in as much detail as possible. (Following up from the last question, Eric goes on to tell me about his shy father and his lovely mum who met at a pub where she was a waitress and he was a regular. After a year of going to see her every day after he got off work, Eric's dad finally got up the nerve to talk to her, blurting out, "Will you marry me?" as he paid his bill one cold, rainy Tuesday. "He was worried if he had made small talk, it might have been another year before he'd get up the nerve to talk to her again," Eric laughs. She didn't say yes that night, but did tell him she'd get a pint with him when her shift was over. When he proposed again six months later, she happily accepted. I loved that Eric told me about his parents in lieu of his own story, clearly valuing his roots as part of his own foundation. He was raised in a loving household and wants nothing more than to make one of his own.)

12. If you could wake up tomorrow having gained any one quality or ability, what would it be? (I hate to admit it, but Eric loses me pretty quickly as he explains he'd like the ability to have a really big breakthrough in his lab at work. He isn't trying too hard to explain it to me though, so I don't feel bad, but maybe one of these days I'll be able to

follow along with what he's talking about.)

"How did I do?" he asks, realizing the line of questioning has finally ceased.

"You did great," I say, smiling and finally relaxed now that I've had some wine and distraction.

"I'll have to come up with my own questions for you," he says. "I could just ask you yours, I suppose, but I'll think it over first."

"I'd love that."

"For tonight, though, may I be so bold as to just ask, your place or mine?"

"You may indeed. And seeing as how you still live below a guy I was just dating, I think we'll stick with mine if that's all right."

Chapter Five

April 10

Maybe it was the great sex after our last date that made me forget about the whole email and extortion thing. Maybe I just really didn't want to remember it. Or maybe it was neither of those things and I'm just the most forgetful person in the world.

Regardless of why I forgot, the fact remains that I forgot. And forgetting felt really good for a few days. Until I wake up this morning to my phone ringing at six, which I wouldn't enjoy under any circumstance, but especially not this one.

"Cyn, it's Sam," I hear, bleary-eyed and cranky.

"You better be dead or dying," I say, my whole not-a-morning-person persona shining through.

"You need to check out Gossip A to Z." She is clearly neither dead nor dying. "It's bad."

I jump out of bed and sit down at my desk to fire up my laptop.

"They were posted in the middle of the night," she says. "My friend at Channel 12 texted me this morning asking for comment."

As the page loads and I see the first few pictures, my heart stops racing and I begin to tell myself it's not that bad. The first picture is of me with Javier holding hands on the sidewalk. I assumed there would be something like that and it's fine. I scroll down to see similar pictures of me with Ken and Peter and a nice shot of me standing alone at the Prom that must have been right before I made my escape.

"These are fine," I say, exhaling loudly. "People know I'm dating different men this year already and I warned the guys. What could be so bad—?"

The next words get stuck in my throat as I scroll down a bit farther and see why Sam sounds so upset. It's not just pictures of me out and about with these three guys. It's the text that goes with it.

> *Local ice cream shop owner Cynthia Blake has been up to some Sinfully Good times lately. After announcing a preposterous plan to date not one, not two, but twelve men this year in the hopes of finding a husband, the desperate Blake is proving good to her word, already leading three men so far down her path of despicable depravity.*
>
> *Sure, a few dates here and there to get to know someone sounds harmless, but Blake and her beaus have been caught in some pretty naughty behavior, including an indecent exposure moment in the backseat of one of the men's cars. How's that for two scoops, Arizona?*

There's a blurry picture of Peter talking to the man who caught us that night and my stomach drops as I look closely and see that I've clearly got my top off. My breasts are covered by the word "WHORE," and I want to throw up.

Is this really how women are finding true love these days? Or is Ms. Blake just out to sleep with as many men as she can this year, which is what it looks like to us. We'll post more pictures soon so you can all meet her April "flavor," as she calls it, but this whole thing is anything but sweet.

"Did you know someone had pictures of you?" asks Sam, who I'd almost forgotten was still on the phone.

"I found out a few days ago," I say, quietly. "They tried to blackmail me. I forgot about it."

"You forgot you were being blackmailed?" She sounds incredulous. "Cyn, that's not something you should forget."

"I didn't forget forget. I guess I didn't really think they'd go through with it. And I didn't think they'd have anything that incriminating. I just thought it would be a little embarrassing."

"I'm sorry, Cyn," Sam says. "I didn't mean to make it sound like it's your fault or anything. It's just not like you to not be all over something that could damage the stores."

She's right and I know it, but the stores were the last thing on my mind as these images came into view. I may not be too embarrassed about a few pictures on a blog, but the three men in the pictures with me have families and careers to consider. And Eric specifically said he'd hate to be involved with anything like this. In one fell swoop, I may have ruined other lives and blown any chance I might have had with a great guy.

I'm filled with self-loathing, so I thank Sam for alerting me and tell her I'll talk to her later. Before I can deal with how shitty I'm feeling, I send a new text to Javier, Ken, and Peter with a link to the blog, an apology, and a note to call me if they want to talk.

It's early, but I know Eric goes into the lab around this time, so I pick up the phone to call him. I try to be like him and rehearse what I'm going to say before he picks up, but he answers almost immediately and I'm still completely unsure of what to say when I hear his kind voice on the other end.

"The pictures are up and it's worse than I thought and I totally understand if you never want to see me again," I say in one breath, opting for the rip-off-the-Band-Aid approach.

"Are you okay?" he says, again sweetly concerned with my well-being over what this might mean.

"Only if you are." I realize as the words come out that it's completely true. I can apologize to the others and make it right however I can. But if this is something Eric can't get past, I will be crushed.

"I'm angry." He goes quiet, and I get the feeling he's thinking things over, maybe wondering how much trouble I'm worth.

"I know and I'm so sorry. I should have paid them, but I'm not even sure that would have worked. I understand if you want to end this."

"Wait, do you think I'm angry with you?"

"Well, yes." I'm unsure of what he means.

"I'm angry at *them*," he says emphatically. "I am livid that someone has invaded your privacy like this and even more so that they've gone after your character. I am furious that there are people in this world who would try to make money from other people's misery. And I'm angry at them for making you worry that something like this could come between us. But you? No, Cynthia, I'm not angry with you at all."

"I wish I could kiss you right now," I say.

"I have to go to work. But I'll stop by on my way and we can snog for a minute if that'll make you feel better."

"It really will." I smile. "And not just because you said snogging and I love that word."

"It felt like the right occasion for it," he says with a laugh. "Now go unlock the door and climb back in bed. I'll come in to kiss you goodbye and we can pretend we're an old married couple who still say goodbye like a couple of teenagers."

"Deal." I get up to do as I'm told.

I get back in bed and try to think about the wonderful man on his way to comfort me instead of everything else I've been focused on this morning. After what feels like only a couple of minutes, I hear the door open and footsteps down the hall and wonder how Eric could have gotten here so fast. Before I can check the time, a familiar shadow darkens my doorway and I nearly gasp.

It's Carter.

*

"I just got off work and had a few texts from friends about that stupid website," he says, clearly out of breath. "I wanted to come see if you're okay. I would have knocked, but the door was open and that made me even more worried for some reason. Judging by the look on your face, you've already seen it."

I'm gaping at him and can't seem to make words come out, but before I can even stop to think about forming words, I jump out of bed and into his arms. Hot, heavy tears are on his shoulder as I sob like a little kid, snot and all. He's changed out of his scrubs and into a soft T-shirt of his that I love, and I move away from the gross shoulder to rest my head on the clean side while I catch my breath.

I'm sure I look horrible, but I can almost see myself through Carter's eyes as I gaze up at him before launching into round two of crying. The expression he has on his face shows nothing of the loathing and ickiness I currently feel about myself. Instead, he just looks worried about me. It hadn't even occurred to me to let him know about all of this, but here he is, showing up to help me through it before he can even decide what it all means to him. My tears take on a new meaning as I start to think about how many hearts I'm leaving in my wake.

"I'm sorry," I say, finally able to form a sentence. It's only two words and not nearly adequate, but it's all I can do right now.

"I know," he says, gently. "I'm sorry too. I thought I could stay away from you and let you do what you need to this year, but maybe…"

I don't get to hear what we could maybe do because at that exact moment, we both turn to see a very confused Eric standing in my hallway. I pull back from Carter's embrace abruptly, once again unable to come up with the right words to say for what might be the world's most awkward situation ever.

Carter looks like I punched him in the gut, and I might as well have. I can't see Eric's expression as clearly, but it looks more confused than hurt, a relief for sure. Staring at both of them in turn, I feel a new resolve building within me. Neither of these men deserves anything less than the whole truth from me at this moment and the only way I can think to tell it is in tandem.

"Let's move this to the kitchen," I say, grabbing Carter's hand and leading him back down the hallway. I grab Eric with my other hand as we go, forcing them to walk side by side behind me. I lead them both to chairs on opposite sides of my dinette set and sit between them.

"Carter, this is Eric," I say. "Eric, this is Carter."

"April?" asks Carter, clearly sizing Eric up.

"Yes," I say. "And Eric—Carter and I were sort of dating before this whole thing started. He and I have plans to date again in June."

"I see," says Eric. "I didn't realize that someone in the mix had a clear advantage."

"Hey—she was dating me when she came up with this whole Plan," says Carter. "I wouldn't say I have any advantage."

"Carter came by to check on me," I continue to explain. "Eric was on his way over to do that same thing. That's why the door was open. I can't tell you both how much it means to me that you are here for me today. You both have reason to be hurt or angry with me, but your showing up this morning tells me you're in this with me and that's more than I deserve."

They both reach out to grab my hand but pull back when they see the other doing the same thing. Seriously, it's so damn awkward in here, but I press on.

"I need some time to figure out what to do about this whole Gossip A to Z thing and I want you both to do the same," I say. "Someone is clearly following me somehow and this could be really embarrassing for anyone involved with me. I will check with my lawyer about getting everything pulled down, but I doubt that's really an option. Sam mentioned this morning that local news outlets are already picking the story up. I will completely understand if you decide you don't want to be with me because of this."

I'm speaking to both of them, so I try to keep looking back and forth, but I can't help myself from staring at Carter a bit longer as I speak. He gave me an opportunity to walk away from all of this and I screwed it all up. This has to be especially painful for him. I hope he gives me a chance to talk with him before our month begins. There's so much more to say.

"I'm not going anywhere," says Eric. "I'll take some time to think about how we move forward like you're asking, but that's exactly what I'll be thinking about. How *we* will move forward."

Carter stands up while speaking and I know he wants me to notice that he's clearly just as in as Eric when he says, "Ditto. I'm not giving up on us."

So there I am, sitting between a prince (okay, not really) and a doctor (also, not quite, but close enough) and facing what could be the greatest or most confusing decision of my life.

I'm still pissed about the website, but something tells me I'll remember today for this moment more than anything else.

Chapter Six

April 11

A quick chat with my lawyer is about as productive as I thought it would be. I can send a letter demanding that the photos be taken down from the Gossip A to Z website and potentially sue them, but the story has already spread like wildfire, and it would be tough to undo the damage. Any lawsuit would probably just garner more media attention anyway. And it would be expensive. I suddenly understand that the people behind this website definitely know what they are doing.

And that's another thing that has me agitated today: who is behind all of this? Covering my Plan is one thing, but there seems to be some real vitriol in the text. It feels personal. Maybe that's because it's happening to me and I feel completely attacked, but something tells me the person or persons involved want to hurt specifically me.

I have no idea how they've been able to get the pictures they've posted, and my only thought is they must have hired a private investigator to follow me. It's a terribly unsettling feeling and I've been peering out of my windows for two days straight trying to catch a glimpse of whoever it could be. If I ever leave my house again, and that's a pretty big if, I'll be looking over my shoulder constantly.

I've heard from Ken and Peter, who mostly find it both mildly amusing and annoying. They've assured me I needn't worry about what this will do to their careers and Ken even went so far as to share that he's already gotten a couple of dates out of it. Figures. I get shamed and he gets laid.

I haven't heard from Javier and he's the one I'm most worried about. As a teacher, I'm sure it's not great for his students to see him online under these circumstances, but at least our picture was relatively innocent. And, since he went first, his seems the most innocuous. He hasn't responded to my texts and neither has Kim, who I'm sure is also finding a renewed sense of anger toward me.

Meg, Eric, and Carter have all been great, and even Sam has been really sweet, bringing me food and updates from the store. Surprisingly, business is booming, and it sounds like customers are so far more curious to try to catch a glimpse of me instead of being turned off by my sinful ways. Or whatever the website is trying to convince them.

I keep having to resist the urge to reply to the email that sent me the photos in the first place, as I know anything I write will just end up posted for all the world to see. It doesn't stop me from opening a draft to vent a bit every few hours, but I haven't hit send on any of them and don't intend to.

I've just finished writing another scathing response I won't send, when I see a new message come in from Jess. In all the hubbub over my former boyfriends, I forgot that I still need to think about my next one. I hold my breath and open the message, bracing myself for a rejection letter in light of everything that's happened.

Dear Cynthia,

I just heard about that awful blog stuff and wanted to see if you're okay. I hate that shit. Sorry for swearing in one of our first communications, but I have no tolerance for people who make money by humiliating others. I just wanted to let you know I'm thinking of you and hope you're still moving for-ward with everything as planned so I can get my chance to take you out next month. Just like Luke said to Lorelai on their first date, "I'm in. I am all in."

Hoping you are too,

Jess

Dear Jess,

Not only am I still definitely in, but I am even more excited to meet you now than I was before. I've never met someone who could quote Gilmore Girls as well as I can. You're definitely earning some points. Oh, and I also can't thank you enough for being so understanding. There's a very real chance that pictures of us may be posted to this ridiculous site over the course of next month. If you're sure you're up for that, I'll see you soon.

Cynthia/Rory

Chapter Seven

April 12

Eric and I had plans to go out tonight, but I'm still too nervous to be out in public and he's too sweet to push me out of my comfort zone. Or maybe he's also not thrilled with the idea of having his picture added to the internet. Either way, we're staying in and that's just fine by me.

I'm excited to see him as he walks in the door, but immediately sense a slight hesitation in his touch as he bends down to kiss me on the cheek.

"You okay?" I say, assuming he's still freaked out by the whole situation.

"I am," he says. "But I'm just a bit freaked out by the whole situation."

I'm a damn psychic.

"I totally understand. I have some ideas for how we can avoid having our picture taken when we're out and about though…"

"Not about that," he interrupts me. "I'm not worried about the website. I mean, I don't love it, but I can handle it."

"Then what's wrong?"

"I knew you'd been dating other guys when this all started," he begins. "But I didn't know you were in love with one of them."

"I was falling for Javier, but that's over. But I'm definitely not in love with any of them."

"No, but unless I'm way off base, you are in love with Carter. And he's in love with you too."

I let the weight of his words sit between us for a moment and try to come up with a response. Do I love Carter? The word "yes" pops into my head before I can even finish thinking the question. I know without a doubt that he loves me too. But the whole point of going through with this thing was to make sure that I love him enough to spend the rest of my life with him, and for him to know without a doubt that I choose him above all others. It's complicated. It's messy. And it's made even more both of those things because of the man standing in front of me.

"Carter and I were casual for years," I say, opting for truth and transparency. "We weren't even really together. I thought about trying to make it work a few times, but he never seemed ready, and I just assumed he saw me as a friend with benefits. When I came up with this whole idea in December, it was because I was tired of not being in a serious relationship. I didn't know it then, but Carter did want to be with me, and he was crushed at the idea of me dating other people at first."

"That's what I thought. So, what happened?"

"I almost called it off when he told me that. But the fact that I'd even come up with this idea in the first place made him think I should go through with it and see if I could find anything better than what we had. He didn't want to be with me knowing I'd always wonder if I made the right choice."

"So, I'm not really competing with eleven other men." He sounds matter of fact. "We're all competing with him."

I hadn't thought about it like that, but I know Eric is right. Haven't I been comparing each of these guys to Carter all along? And don't I feel less pressure to make one of them work, knowing I have a great guy to fall back on?

"That's not what I intended," I say. "But it does seem to be working out that way."

"And how am I comparing so far?" He looks pained.

I smile and hope both my words and tone can help ease his mind.

"You are wonderful, and I am so, so thankful to have found you. I was so worried that all this publicity was going to drive you away. I didn't care about anything else when I saw it. Not me, not the stores. Well, I cared about hurting the other people involved, but really, it was the thought of losing you that made me so heartsick."

He nods and puts his head in his hands for a minute. I can tell this is all really weighing on him and hope with all my might that he feels like I'm worth it in the end. I have no idea why he would, but all I can do is hope.

"We've been dating two weeks," he says, picking his head back up to look at me. "I shouldn't be putting all this pressure on you. Got any more Disney movies to show me to lighten the mood?"

"Heck yes, I do," I say with a laugh.

Eric pulls me in for a hug and I can feel the tension leave his body as I melt into his arms. We've had a few of these tough conversations over the past couple days and I hope we can both relax enough to let a movie distract us into a lighter mood.

I opt for *The Little Mermaid* and excitedly point at the screen the first time Prince Eric comes into view.

"I had the biggest crush on him when I was a kid," I say, giggling. "And now I have my very own, real-life version in you!"

"Well, since we're confessing cartoon character crushes," says Eric, laughing, "I guess I should admit that Ariel was always pretty high on the list for me. Something about that seashell bra, I guess."

"I can see that." I lean into his arms as we sit side by side on the couch and thank my lucky stars once again for the power of Disney Magic this month and always.

Chapter Eight

www.flavorsofthemonth.bloggerific.com

As you all probably know by now, photos of myself and the men I've dated so far this year have been made public with some not-so-nice comments attached to them. I would ask that you please respect the privacy of these kind, wonderful men who do not deserve any sort of backlash from all of this.

As for me, I will neither be embarrassed by nor apologize for my actions and hope you all still know my heart is in the right place both personally and professionally. I am not sure what caused the people behind a local tabloid to target me, but I'm sure they are getting thousands of clicks for their content, so I suppose I do have a good idea why they'd do it.

If you'd like to continue your search for love, we'll be hosting another speed dating event this month. No paparazzi will be

*in attendance, so feel free to get to know each other in a safe,
comfortable environment. Even if you don't find a love
connection, you'll get some ice cream, so that's still a pretty
good night.*

April 15

I 've never been a big fan of showing up places unannounced, but I wasn't sure how else to talk to Kim. I'm outside of her house with bagels, champagne, and orange juice and hoping the promise of mimosas will get her to open the door. I hold my breath and knock.

I hear her feet shuffle to the door and know she's looking at me through the peephole, so I smile my best "I come here in peace" smile and wait. She opens the door, stares at me blankly, and finally says, "Oh, fine. You better have the cream cheese I like."

Because I am not an idiot, I absolutely do have the cream cheese she likes, so I walk in and set everything down in her kitchen. I want to take things slowly, so I don't say anything as I pull everything I've brought out of the bags, grab some glasses from her cabinets, and fix us a pretty nice little meal. I make the mimosas just how we like them (mostly champagne with a splash of juice) and I sit down at the table, gesturing for her to do the same.

"Are you in love with Javier?" I say, still on my whole blunt and truthful kick.

"I was going to ask you the same question," she says.

"I thought I might be. But if there's even a small chance that you are, consider those feelings ancient history."

"It's not your feelings I'm super worried about right now." She looks on the verge of tears.

I sit and listen as she tells me she had feelings for Javier pretty much the moment she met him but was worried about the whole dating a coworker thing. Watching him date me was really hard and she began to resent me the more time I spent with him.

"I know it's not fair because I was the one who introduced you," she says. "But I couldn't help it. Seeing you so happy with him was hard enough but knowing you could see how great he was and then continue to date eleven other men killed me."

I nod sympathetically as she continues. She thought I would end the whole thing when it was clear I was falling for him, but when I slept with Carter, then acted like Javier being ready to propose wasn't even a big deal, she went from hurt to pissed.

"I called Javier and asked if we could meet so that we could talk about everything that had happened," she says. "I let him talk about you and tried to find a time to tell him how I feel, but he was so heartbroken that I couldn't get the words out. I was one of the few people in his life who knew about you two, so I became the person he'd talk to when he was feeling down. I thought that maybe if I was a good friend, he'd eventually start to see me as something more."

Javier had seemed like he was getting over me, so Kim decided to casually ask him out. The Prom supports a lot of the programs he likes to volunteer with, so she invited him to be her date, knowing I'd be there with Peter.

"I thought if he saw you there with another man, he'd really understand that you had moved on," she continued. "It's one thing to hear that you're out with someone else, but to see it in person is even harder. I'm not sure what I was thinking. He did see you with Peter and seemed even more crushed. And then we both saw you leave with someone else, and he didn't say a word. We haven't talked about you since."

"Is that why you told Ken I was falling for him?" I ask.

"Yes," she admits. "I actually did think you really liked him, but I also thought that if you could get over Javier quickly, you might let him go and he could begin to heal. I was worried about him, but I was also hopeful for me."

"I'm so sorry. I'm sorry I dated Javier in the first place."

"No, I'm sorry. I never should have set you up with him, given how I felt about him. He's such a great guy. How could you not fall for him? And how could he not fall for you?"

"I can think of a few reasons."

"Don't let that stupid tabloid shit make you doubt yourself," she says, forcefully. "You are awesome, they are dumb, and you know the truth about this whole thing. You weren't trying to hurt anyone."

There's the Kim I know and love. She's on my side again and I feel stronger already.

"I wasn't trying to," I say, "but that doesn't mean people still didn't get hurt. And welcome back, friend."

"It's good to be back."

We sip our mimosas, nibble on our bagels, and catch up about other things that have been going on with each other. I fill her in on Peter and she laughs her head off about the whole mix-up thing. She asks me about Eric and notices immediately that I take on a different demeanor when I talk about him. My feelings are clearly betraying me, but she doesn't press me for more information.

"I can't believe he took you to Disneyland that night," she says, smiling. "He sounds pretty perfect."

I nod, realizing there's not a single negative thing I can say about him. That's probably true for a lot of people you've only known two weeks though, right?

"I don't know what to do," I confess. "I have two guys right now who I think could be really great. How do I choose?"

"Well, if you're not sure which of them to choose, I think you need to keep moving forward with the Plan. It'll add more choices to the mix, but maybe you'll get some clarity along the way. Plus, if you can't choose between Carter and Eric, maybe that means neither of them is the one for you. Wouldn't it be more obvious if it were?"

"I have no idea," I admit. "I had no idea how Carter was feeling all those years, so who am I to act like an expert on this topic?"

"Yeah, you're not great at noticing things, are you?"

We both laugh, but my heart quickens as I think again about the fact that someone has been following me these last few months without me noticing. Could I be any less perceptive?

"Hey," she says, seeing my face fall. "None of this crap with the website is your fault, okay? And nothing they can post about you can dull your sparkle. You are Cynthia Fucking Blake, successful business-woman and all-around badass. You are going to end this year with your head held high and hopefully your hand weighed down by a new, important piece of jewelry. And when we find out who is behind this whole mess, they'll have to answer to me."

I jump up, pull Kim to her feet, and wrap her up in a hug so tight I'm worried I might hurt her. "And Javier will come around," I whisper in her ear. "If he knows what's good for him."

"Damn right he will." She's trying to sound strong and tough, but a crack in her voice betrays the emotions I know she's fighting to hold back. I let her go and we both stand there for a second, happy to have mended this rift so we can move forward. "So, tell me," she says, eyebrows raised, "how is Prince Eric in bed?"

"I'll tell you after tonight. I mean, I already know, but I have something planned that I think is either the best or worst idea of my life."

*

I 've talked to Eric a few times today over text to confirm where his lab is and that he'll be alone there tonight, but I'm a nervous wreck as I pull into a parking space right next to his car. And not just because I can barely walk in what I'm wearing. That's definitely a concern, but what if he thinks I'm an idiot for what I've got planned? I should really just drive home.

I look down at myself for the hundredth time and decide to go for it. I look sexy and this will be fun. It will be. Fun, not crazy. Here goes nothing.

I step out of the car and take tiny steps all the way to the door, then text him so that he can buzz me into the building. I can barely move in this outfit and I'm trying to slow my breathing, afraid I'll walk into his lab a sweaty mess. I've got a long coat over the whole ensemble, and this wig is making me really hot. Maybe I should go back.

The door buzzes and I decide it would be rude to leave, so I open it and walk down the hall, looking for the door number he told me. It's all the way at the end, of course, and I have to take another minute to catch my breath before I open it and walk inside.

Eric is sitting at a desk, hunched over piles of paperwork and clearly looking for something.

"Just one sec," he says without looking up. "I need to find this one last thing and then I'm all yours. Aha—there it is. Now, how are you…"

He's picked up a packet of papers triumphantly and looks up at last, but stops mid-sentence when he sees me. I've dropped the coat and am trying to strike a sexy pose, but I can't tell if it's having the right effect. His jaw is still hanging slack, and I'm about to bend down for the coat when his face changes to the biggest smile I've seen on it so far.

"Well, well, well," he says, rubbing his hands together. "And what are you doing so far from the sea?"

"I came to rescue my handsome prince," I say, doing my best Ariel impression to go with the costume I'm wearing. With a long, red wig, purple seashell bra, and skintight green sparkly skirt, I'm hoping I've created the fun fantasy he's always dreamed of.

"Rescue away, my dear," he says, clearly amused.

I start to take a few steps toward him, but he quickly comes to pick me up, seeing how hard it is for me to walk in this get-up.

"Guess I'll be the one doing the rescuing," he says with a laugh, carrying me over to one of the long desks. With one sweeping movement, he throws everything to the floor and sets me down. He takes another second to look down at me before leaning in to kiss me urgently.

"How do we turn you from a mermaid to a person?" he says. "Your fins are very much in my way at the moment."

"Hold on," I say, standing up to face him. "There was one thing I wanted to do for you while I'm still a mermaid."

I ease myself down onto my knees in front of him and start taking off his belt. He laughs, but I can tell that somewhere, in a memory he's never told anyone, he definitely fantasized about getting a blowjob from Ariel. I'm not sure why, but I'm suddenly certain every man his age did. So that's what I do.

Maybe it's the costume or maybe it's just because I'm really good at it, but it takes all of about a minute to get him off. I laugh as he pulls me back to a standing position, but he's too preoccupied with the zipper on my skirt to mind. He finds it and begins inching it down my hips and thighs, sighing when he realizes I'm not wearing anything under it. I step out of it, now wearing nothing but the wig, bra, heels, and a big smile as he picks me back up to put me back onto the desk. He sits me there just barely, so that I'm mostly hanging off the end.

He pushes me back gently to make sure I'm right where he wants me. Eric drops to his knees and moves my legs apart so that he can return the favor. And oh, does he. His face is between my thighs, and I feel tingly immediately as he kisses, licks, and fingers me to oblivion. He stands back up as I quiver and presses his dick inside me to feel the end of my orgasm from the inside.

I'm impressed that he's able to go again so quickly, assuming that a fantasy from his adolescence is bringing out the teenager in him. But as he eases himself in and out of me expertly, I remember with a smile that no high school or even college guy ever had moves like this.

Beads of sweat come down from my neck and pool in my seashells, but I don't want to take off the wig while he's enjoying everything so much. I lean back slowly onto the table so that I'm now lying down completely while he continues to fuck me.

"You're so hot," he says, looking down at me.

"I knew you'd like it," I say.

"No, I mean, you look like you're burning up. Come here."

We stop for a second while he stands me back up and I take off the wig and plastic bra. The air hitting my skin feels amazing, especially on the back of my neck, which is also covered in sweat. Eric turns me around and begins blowing gently at me, helping me to cool down. I put my hands down on the table, loving the feeling of the cool air on my back, and smile as Eric enters me from behind, apparently satisfied that I'm not about to pass out.

We finish in that position, but Eric turns me around to hold me in his arms and kiss me sweetly.

"That was amazing," he says. "You're amazing. No one has ever dressed up like a Disney Princess and shown up at my work so that I can have sex with her before."

"I should hope not," I say with a laugh. "I'd hate to think I'm un-original."

Chapter Nine

April 15

I 'm filling in Kim and Meg about my stint as a Disney Princess as we hike, and we all decide we'd better sit for a second to catch our breath before we go tumbling down the mountain. It's not that we're not in shape or anything, but they're now both laughing so hard and clutching their sides that I'm worried one or both of them might faint.

"I…cannot…believe…you…did…that…" Meg says through bouts of laughter.

"Careful, preggo," says Kim. "You're hiking for two."

"You can totally believe I did that," I say, getting a few big gulps of air as we step to the side of the trail. "What I can't believe is that I told you about it. I must be crazy."

"Nah, you just wanted to impress a prince," says Meg, reaching back for the water bottle I'm handing her. "And what better way to do that than pretending to be a princess?"

We laugh again and look out over the city. We're about halfway up Piestewa Peak, but we've already got a pretty decent view of Phoenix. It's early and it rained last night, so the city is clear and shiny. It's pretty great. Plus, I've got my two best friends back and a couple of great guys who really care about me. Everything seems perfect until I flash for a moment to the awful things being said about me online.

There's only been one Gossip A to Z post, but Sam says she's getting several calls from other media outlets every day at the stores. Our social media pages have also started getting comments about everything, ranging from some trolls who pretty much agree with the initial post to some nice customers who defend me. I try to stay out of it, but it's hard not to scroll through and see what's being said.

I'm pushing myself back up off the rock I have been sitting on to focus on our hike when I see it. Just below us on the trail is a man with one of those big cameras with a long lens pointed right at me. Kim sees him too, and we both look at each other for a second.

"Is that...?" I start to ask.

"Stay with Meg," she says, handing me her water bottle. "I'm faster than you."

Before I can protest, Kim is scurrying back down the trail, heading right for the guy with the camera. He sees her and turns around, nearly knocking over a couple of hikers as he begins his rapid descent. They're both soon out of my view, so Meg and I head down after them, but much slower and cautiously. The trail is a bit wet, making some of the rocks slippery, so we take our time, muttering to each other that we hope Kim is being careful.

By the time we get to the base of the mountain, Kim is walking back toward us, looking about as angry as I've ever seen her.

"He got away," she says, kicking a rock. "I slipped and it slowed me down. I'm sorry, Cyn."

"It's okay," I reassure her. "As long as you're okay. Did you get a look at him? Or see what kind of car he was driving?"

"He had a hat and sunglasses," she says. "And I didn't see him get into a car. I heard one speeding away when I got there though, so I assume that was him. And yes, I'm fine. Just a little scrape on my hand and leg."

"It's six-thirty in the morning," says Meg. "How in the world did he know we'd be here?"

We all stand there silently for a minute, and I hate to see how distraught Kim and Meg look at the thought of someone following us all. It's been creepy enough for me to deal with, but they're just starting to realize how awful it feels.

"I really hate these people," says Kim, sounding defiant. "I wish I could have caught up to that guy."

"I'm kinda glad you didn't," I say, laughing. "I'm not really in the mood to bail you out of jail for assaulting a man with his own camera."

"That's exactly what I was planning." Kim trades her anger for a sarcastic smile. "How'd you know?"

"You're resourceful," I fire back. "And it only makes sense to use the bad guy's weapon against him."

I stand between them both, putting an arm around each of them, and lead us back to my car.

"Breakfast is on me," I say. "I'd say it's the least I can do after getting you both stalked by a stranger."

Chapter Ten

April 18

I call Eric to tell him about the photographer on the mountain and he is both worried for me and eager to comfort me, just like I hoped he would be. He asks what I'd like to do for the rest of the day, and I realize it's coming up on the end of April and I haven't been to a Diamondbacks game yet this season.

"Take me out to the ballgame?" I say, wondering if British people know the words to that song.

"I'll even buy you some peanuts and crackerjack," he says. "But I have to warn you now: I don't actually know much about baseball. I may ask some pretty dumb questions."

I change into a D-backs shirt, hat, and shorts and head over to pick Eric up. On my way to his apartment, I run into Peter and Cara, who are also walking from the parking lot toward his building.

"Uh, hi," says Peter. "What are you doing here?"

"Oh, hi," I say back. "I'm actually here to pick up a friend. Hi, Cara. Nice to see you."

"Oh, hey, Cynthia," says Cara.

Under normal circumstances, this would be where I'd ask Cara a few questions about what she's been up to the last fifteen years, but I'm pretty sure she knows about Peter and me and I have very little desire to prolong this encounter. I let them walk ahead of me on the path with a "guess I'll see you around," and they nod, grateful for the chance to escape.

As I get to Eric's door, I accidentally think about Peter and Cara hooking up and am especially excited to see him as he answers.

"Well, hello there," he says. "Welcome to my humble abode."

"Oh right." I step inside. "I forgot that I haven't actually seen your place."

My elation at seeing him immediately fades as I take a look around. It's not that the place is messy, thank goodness. Quite the opposite. It looks like no one actually lives here. There are a couple of pieces of furniture, but it's very sparse and cold.

"I know it's not much to look at," he says with a shrug, clearly understanding the shift in my mood. "But I wasn't sure how long I'd even be here, so I didn't bother with decorating. And I'm at the lab so much that it's never really bothered me, but I can tell it must look pretty sad to you."

"No, no," I say, not wanting him to feel bad. "It's fine and that makes sense. It just caught me by surprise."

And that's true, but there's something else bugging me that I can't quite put my finger on. Arizona is home to me, and I love it here, but seeing how Eric lives, it seems clear all of a sudden that it's not home to him. I have never even thought to ask him what his plans for the future are because it seemed too early. But now, looking around, I think I may have an answer. This is not the home of someone looking to put down roots. This is a temporary stop. And I want to cry.

"So, I don't actually have any Diamondbacks gear," he says, clearly wanting to change the subject. "But I thought if I just wore this plain, white T-shirt, you could help me shop for something when we get there."

"Perfect," I say, 100 percent on board with the idea that we should talk about something else. "Let's go."

We fall into easy conversation in the car, especially after I tell Eric about running into Peter and Cara on the way to his apartment.

"Is it weird to see him with her?" he asks me.

"Kinda, but probably not for the reason you're thinking," I say.

I delicately tell Eric that Peter and I never really slept together during our month and do my best to not fully explain why. Peter was a nice guy and there's no reason to disparage him to another man, but I'm pretty sure Eric can guess at what I'm saying.

"So, I'm less embarrassed to see him with another woman because we weren't really that intimate," I say, "but more embarrassed because I know what she's dealing with."

Eric laughs at this, and I break into giggles too, but then I cut us off. "Now, now, we really shouldn't be laughing at this. It's not his fault."

"You're right." Eric is trying to keep a straight face. "What we should be laughing about is how you escaped from his room down a tree one day and then peed in the sprinklers another day. Trying to escape his tiny penis, were you?"

I don't know whether to laugh or cry, so I go for both options as we pull into the parking garage at Chase Field.

"You never told me you knew that's what I was doing," I shriek, trying to drive, laugh, and cry all at the same time.

"Well, I didn't know why until just now," he says, nearly doubled over with laughter himself. "I thought maybe he was a jerk and had tried to hurt you or something and I didn't want you to feel worse. But if it's all because you were too nice to tell him he's got a small pecker, I feel like it's fair game."

We are cracking up as I turn off the car and we sit there for a second trying to catch our breath.

"You won't ever tell anyone about that, will you?" I say.

"Er, I won't tell anyone else." He pulls a face. "I didn't know I'd ever meet you and I may have told a coworker…and my mum."

"Oh geez." I turn scarlet with mortification. "I hope they never make the connection between that crazy girl and me."

"I think you're safe." He takes my hand as we walk toward the stadium. "Now, where's the best place to get me some team spirit? I'm going to be the biggest Diamondbacks fan ever by the time this game is over. How long are baseball games, then? Ninety minutes?"

"Nine innings."

"And how long is an inning?" he asks, clearly ready to learn everything he can.

"They aren't timed. Each team gets a chance to bat and keeps going until they get three outs."

He seems very confused by the notion that a baseball game could go on forever, and I laugh as I try to explain that it will eventually end. We cover the different positions on the field and how many strikes, balls, and outs each team gets, but he looks thoroughly confused as we walk into the Team Shop.

"Here," I say, picking up a program. "There's a sheet in here we can use to keep score. I'll teach you how and it will make more sense as we watch."

"Deal," he says, looking around at the walls. "I think I'll get one of those jerseys. Which player should I get?"

"Well," I begin, "there are a lot of good players, but you don't know any of them yet. Do you want me to just tell you my favorite one?"

"Nah, I have an idea." He grabs a blank jersey in his size and walks it up to the counter where they add the letters.

I go to the assortment of hats along the wall and look around for one I think he might like. I've never seen him in a ball cap but I bet he'll look adorable. I've narrowed it down to three when he comes up behind me to show me his new threads.

"What do you think?" he says, turning around so I can see the whole thing. And there, on his back, is the word "Prince" in Sedona Red letters.

"Very nice, my prince," I say, smiling.

"I thought you'd like that." He turns around to smile at me.

"Now everyone's going to think I'm here with royalty. I'll have to fight the ladies off with a stick."

"Don't worry." He pulls me close to whisper in my ear. "You're the only one who's ever gone down on me while pretending to be a princess. I don't think anyone here or anywhere could steal me away."

I laugh and push him away from me for a second so I can try the different hats I've grabbed on him to see which one looks best. He lets me pick one and I buy it and the program so we can go find our seats.

I spend the game teaching Eric all about baseball and by the third inning, he's keeping score on his own, with my help and guidance, as different scenarios come up. I've also taught him the subtle art of chewing and spitting out sunflower seeds, finding the best food in the ballpark, and drinking a beer in the middle of the afternoon because we can.

During the seventh inning stretch, we sing along to "Take Me Out to the Ballgame," and Eric says he has no idea why he knows the words, but he must have picked it up from American television through the years. He's completely gotten the hang of keeping score by this point and I am thrilled to see that he seems to be enjoying himself. The game ends in a walk-off double, so I'm feeling pretty great as we leave our seats and head out on the concourse.

We're tipsy and a little giddy as we walk toward a bar down the street to grab another drink. As we walk, I feel my pocket vibrate. Then again. Then again. I don't usually check my phone on dates, but it's buzzing quite a bit now and I apologize to Eric as I pull it out to see what's going on. It's a series of texts that just keeps getting worse.

Sam: Did you see gossipaz?

Sam: Look (link)

Sam: Did you see anyone this time?

Sam: They might still be there. Look around.

The link takes me to a short post with a picture of Eric and me from about thirty minutes ago. I know it can't be from long ago because the picture shows us in our seats with no one in front of us and the people sitting there left in the eighth inning. The text is short, but certainly not sweet.

Out and about with man number four, Cynthia Blake just can't seem to get enough. Even after getting her January suitor fired, it seems like Ms. Blake will keep going with her selfish Plan, no matter who she hurts. If I were her, I'd nip this in the butt.

I quickly scan the area to see if anyone is currently taking our picture as I hand my phone to Eric so he can see what's going on. He looks furious, but thankfully not at me. And even if he were mad at me, he couldn't be as mad as I am at myself. I got Javier fired? I cost a wonderful teacher his job? What the hell is wrong with me?

"Come on," says Eric. "Let's get you home."

I lean into his arms as he leads me to a side street and requests an Uber to pick us up. I'm sick to my stomach, and not just from the ridiculous amount of food and beer we had at the game. The Plan has to stop. And I have to talk to Javier.

*

I call Kim from the car and tell her to check the link I just sent her.

"Is it true?" I say, holding back tears. "Did Javier lose his job over this?"

"Cynthia, no," she says. "He didn't. They're lying."

"Are you sure? When was the last time you talked to him?"

"Uh, well, he's kinda here now." I can hear the smile in Kim's voice. "Want me to ask him if he's just lost his job and hasn't told me?"

I can hear Javier say "huh?" in the background and breathe a huge sigh of relief.

"Look, I don't know why someone would lie about that," says Kim, "but only end this whole thing now if you're really done. Javier is fine. We've been talking and I'll fill you in later, but trust me, he's fine."

"Thanks," I say. "I'll talk to you later."

We hang up and I fill Eric in on the parts of the conversation he couldn't hear. He seems genuinely relieved to hear that Javier didn't lose his job, but our relief quickly turns to the general anger and embarrassment the post has caused in the first place.

"Are you okay?" I ask. "It's the first time your picture has been posted in this whole thing. How are you feeling?"

"Eh, not great," he says. "It's just so crazy to think someone was that close to us, taking our picture without our knowledge. The whole thing is just wrong."

"I agree." We pull up to Eric's apartment complex and I get out to walk him back to his sad one-bedroom.

"Actually," he says, turning to face me on the path to his building, "I think I could use a night on my own if you don't mind. All that food and invasion of privacy has me feeling a bit queasy."

"I totally understand," I say, realizing I also don't feel great. "Maybe a good night's sleep will do us both some good."

After I get home that night from my second Uber ride of the evening, my head swims with more thoughts than any one brain should have to process at a time. I decide it's not a great time to deal with it all, so I hit the hay early and hope that things look better in the morning.

Chapter Eleven

April 19

When I wake up the next morning, I have no new answers, but at least I've gotten some sleep. Eric didn't text me on his way into work and I decide not to read anything into his decision. He's been doing that most days, but there's something about having your picture splashed all over the internet that probably makes you not want to contact the person responsible for it first thing in the morning. I get it.

I spend the day trying to talk myself into going to the gym or doing something productive, but I fail miserably and end up binge-watching TV shows and trying not to think the thoughts that are swarming around me like gnats.

Should I end this all now? I could leave that horrible website with nothing to post about me and potentially move forward with the love of my life if I call everything off. Even if I'm not sure which guy I want to end up with, I don't need to make it this complicated. But does Eric even want to keep dating me at this point? He explicitly said he'd never want to be involved with anything that could get him written about in tabloids. And after the first time it happened, he opts to not only not spend the night with me but avoids me today as well. That seems like a pretty clear answer.

I've got myself pretty convinced I should call Carter and see what he thinks about all of this when my phone buzzes and my heart leaps.

> *Eric: Sorry I haven't reached out all day. I slept in and barely made it to work on time. But you're all I'm thinking about today. Can you come by and see me?*

Per usual, I've made something out of nothing. My mind immediately jumps to the last time I visited Eric in his lab, and I feel better for the first time all day. That's probably not what he has in mind, but the memory of it is enough to perk me up and get my ass off the couch.

> *Me: Of course. Let me make myself presentable and I'll see you soon.*

A mentally strong, smart, grown-up person would spend some time figuring things out before opting to be distracted. I am, however, weak and in no mood to keep sorting through this avalanche of feelings. I take a quick shower, throw on some jeans and a tank top, grab my purse, and leave all the negativity of the past twenty-four hours behind as I walk out the door.

All those thoughts of ending this whole experiment suddenly

sound like the right thing to do, but it's not Carter on my mind as I walk to my car. It's the man I'm on my way to see. I can't help smiling whenever I think of him, and I make a promise to myself that I should at least see if he's at all on the same page tonight. After some good, old-fashioned distraction sex, that is.

I'm not in costume this time as I pull up to the lab, but I'm pretty sure Eric and I can have some fun there as ourselves. I push the door open as he buzzes me in and walk the long hallway down to his door. He's there to open it as I arrive, and he pulls me into a fast embrace.

"We did it," he says, excitedly. "We did it!"

"Yay!" I cry. "I'm so happy! But, er, what did we do?"

"We got the grant we've been hoping for." I realize that the "we" he's referring to is not him and me. "Allen and I have been on the verge of a breakthrough for years and this money is what we'll need to finish our research. Remember? I told you we'd been stuck for a while now."

I do remember this and am so proud and excited for him that I can't even help what comes out of my mouth next.

"I love you," I say. It has nothing to do with the grant, but I realize I've been thinking it for a while now. Seeing him so ecstatic about his job is just another facet of my love for him and I don't want to hold it back anymore.

"You do?" he says, momentarily coming down from his post-grant excitement.

I nod. "I really do."

Eric picks me up and spins me around, laughing so excitedly he almost sounds crazy.

"This is the best day of my life," he nearly shouts, putting me back on the ground. "The grant is exciting, but the woman I love loves me too. How could this day get any better?"

I smile, relieved but not surprised to hear that he feels the same way.

"I have an idea." I take a page from his playbook and throw all the papers off the nearest desk and pull my shirt off over my head. Eric closes the space between us and kisses me passionately.

"I love you, Cynthia," he says in between kisses. "Not sure I officially said it."

"I got the gist," I say, reaching down to unbutton his pants.

We're making out and undressing each other furiously when we hear someone clear their throat nearby.

"Sorry to interrupt, kids," says the throat clearer. "But I figured you'd want to know I'm in the room before having sex on my desk."

I press myself up against Eric to block my topless self and every drop of blood in my body rises to my face. I can only imagine what shade of red I am at this very moment.

"You want to turn your back for a minute, mate?" says Eric, but I can see over his shoulder that the man already has. I take the opportunity to quickly put my bra and shirt back on while we both try to make ourselves presentable. As soon as we are, Eric takes my hand and walks me over to the corner where our interrupter is still turned away from us.

"Allen, this is Cynthia," he says. Allen turns around and I can see by his eyes that he's every bit as embarrassed as we are.

"Pleasure to meet you, Cynthia," says Allen. "And sorry for the circumstances. I knew Eric would be excited about the grant, but I didn't know he'd be *this* excited."

We all laugh as I shake Allen's hand, realizing this is Eric's lab partner who came out from England with him.

"Congratulations," I say. "And sorry about all that. Not sure what came over us."

"It's fine," says Allen jovially. "I'd been meaning to clean out my workspace anyway. You did me a favor, actually. It'll be easier to close this place down."

"Oh," I say, looking between Eric and Allen, "will you be switching labs?"

"Actually," says Eric, looking slightly deflated for the first time since I got here today. "We're switching continents."

"Didn't he tell you?" asks Allen. "The grant requires us to do our work in London. We're going home!"

*

All the air leaves my body as I stare back and forth between Eric and Allen, wondering if this is all some weird joke.

"You're leaving?" Suddenly, the bare apartment and dodged answers on the future all make sense. Eric was never planning to be here long-term. I should have seen it coming. I should have asked.

"Er, I should probably be going," says Allen, clearly not wanting to be present for what's coming next. I bet the thought of walking in on two people having sex isn't looking so bad anymore. He grabs a couple of things from the ground where I dumped them and leaves.

I can't believe I just told Eric I love him. I do, and this doesn't change that, but watching him leave is going to be so much harder now. And how can he say he loves me too, when he's been planning to leave all this time?

It's like the whole world is spinning as the questions I was keeping at bay come back all at once.

"I don't know what to say," he says, pulling me into his arms. "I didn't think this would all happen so fast."

"Me, or the grant?" I say, as my eyes begin to well up.

"Both. We didn't know if it would take months or even years to secure the funding, and when it came, we didn't know where we'd have to do the work. I didn't see the point in telling you. And how could I have known we'd fall so fast for each other?"

His words make sense and I let myself relax a little more into his arms. I have so many more things I want to ask, but for the moment, just being held by him seems like the only right thing in the world.

"Remember when I said I'd like to ask you my own questions?"

Eric says, holding back tears in his own eyes while I let a few of mine fall.

I nod, remembering back to the night where I had really started falling for him in earnest.

"Well, I wrote a few of them down, but now there's only one that matters. Will you abandon this whole plan and move to London with me?"

Holy. Fucking. Shit.

Chapter Twelve

April 30

"Cynthia?" says Eric, from what sounds like ten miles away. "Did you hear what I just said?"

I did hear him. I've heard everything said in this lab tonight, but hearing and processing are two different things. I honestly cannot believe he is leaving, nor can I fathom that he has asked me to go with him. I can't leave my home and move to England. Can I?

"I, uh," I stammer, trying to at least acknowledge that I have, in fact, heard his crazy words. "Heard you. Yes. Heard you."

"That was a lot to spring on you," he says gently. "I don't expect an answer right away. But that's where my head is and I know it's where my heart is. I want to be with you and I think you'd love London. But I've had time to think this all through and you're just hearing it for the first time. I have to leave for London to accept the grant and get a few things set up, but I'll be back to close everything down here and to give a commencement speech in two weeks. Can I ask you to put your Plan on hold while I'm away and not see any more men for the time being?"

So many words and new things to process. I feel like I'm going to faint. My head pings with the word "Jess," but Eric does sound reasonable and if the whole point of this thing was to find someone I could be with, having two great men say they love me feels like a victory. And two weeks isn't such a long time. I nod. It seems my head, at least, has made a decision and is ready to respond.

"Great," he says. "I know it's not what you were thinking for how this year would go, but the thought of you with another guy right now just kills me. Especially now that I know you love me too."

With those words, my brain kicks back on and I realize what I'm facing: only the biggest decisions of my life. Moving to London would not only mean uprooting my whole life, but it would mean closing the door on the possibility of anyone else for the time being, or maybe forever. It would mean choosing Eric over Carter, something I'm not remotely ready to do.

On the other hand, it's a clear path forward where everything else in my life feels murky and confusing. Here is a man who is so sure about me that he knows within a month not only does he love me but wants to make space in his life for me. Carter and I had years of confusion, and it wasn't until he realized he could lose me that he spoke up.

What if I was just a backup for him?

"I will think like I've never thunk before," I tell him. "Thought before. Whatever. Just know that I will be doing some big thinking while you are away. If you change your mind while you're back in Jolly Old England, I need you to tell me right away though, okay?"

"Deal," he says, pulling me in for a hug. "Not going to happen, but deal."

And with that, we walk out of the lab together, but I drive myself home alone to get busy on that whole thinking thing. I know I'm going to need some help on this from Meg and Kim, but for tonight, I decide to give my brain a rest so it can be ready for the crazy volume of thoughts it's about to be hit with.

I dream of tidal waves and tornadoes, which I assume is because my brain feels like a natural disaster. Around 2:00 a.m., I wake up, panting, with the strong suspicion that I am forgetting something. Again, the ping in my brain signals the word "Jess," and I realize I have a date set up for tonight that I forgot to cancel after the whole lab incident. It's certainly too late now, and I really should at least go and break things off in person. I fall back to sleep feeling uneasy and go on with the restlessness.

This time though, I'm rescued from the middle of a storm by a faceless hero; someone strong, smart, and exceedingly kind. I don't know who it is, but I'm too grateful for the break in the deluge to care. Maybe it's me, or one of my friends, or maybe even someone I've dated, but as my alarm wakes me up on the first day of May, I know that is

the feeling I want to be chasing.

Chapter Thirteen

May 1

I'm back to feeling like a total asshole again. I really should have picked up the phone to cancel my date with Jess tonight, but I want a chance to explain everything and apologize, so here I sit. We decided to meet for dinner at a French restaurant in Scottsdale and I'm in the lobby wearing my best "sorry for being a jerk" ensemble. Maybe I should buy Jess dinner? If I quickly blurt out that it's not really a date, that doesn't betray my promise to Eric, right?

As I argue the semantics with myself, I scan the room for someone who looks like they might also be scanning the room. Jess knows what I look like, so I have no idea what I'm looking for, but my head immediately pops to a picture of Milo Ventimiglia, who played Jess on *Gilmore Girls*. If that's actually who shows up, this is going to be even harder than I thought.

That black hair and smolder might be enough to make me break my promise to Eric, I think with a laugh. It's just the asshole version of me talking, but at least she's funny.

I'm a few minutes early, so I walk to the bar for a glass of wine while I wait. I'm still searching faces, which seems pointless, but then I remember I've also been stalked lately, giving me a second reason to give the room a look. I see no cameras nor cell phones pointed at me as I sit and sip my pinot noir, but suddenly I do see a pair of smoldering dark eyes locking onto mine from across the room. They're partially hidden under black hair that is pushed aside as their owner smiles and makes their way toward me.

"Cynthia?" the mouth belonging to the eyes says to me.

"Can I help you?" I scan the hand reaching out to me for signs of a camera or phone. Seeing none, I lock back on the eyes and I'm momentarily dazzled. Are they smoldering back at me, or is it just my imagination?

"I'm Jess," says the owner of the eyes.

"Jess?" I feel faint for the second time in two days.

"It's short for Jessamyn. And judging by the look on your face, I forgot to mention I'm a woman."

"I, er, I just assumed." I'm discovering that stammering and feeling faint go hand in hand for me.

"I think our table is ready." She gestures back toward the hostess. "Why don't we go sit and chat?"

"That would be great." I follow her back through the bar and into the lobby. We are seated at a booth near the back of the restaurant and Jessamyn orders herself a glass of wine from our server then faces me with a gentle smile.

"Your posts said that you wanted to find someone to spend the rest of your life with," she begins. "I thought you might want to explore all of your options. But honestly, I really love ice cream and I thought the worst thing that would happen is we each get a new friend and I maybe get a few free scoops."

I laugh, louder and harder than I normally would in a nice restaurant and immediately feel at ease with Jess, if not a bit confused by the turn of events. But, seeing as I was coming out tonight for a date with no intention of dating the person, this is probably going to be equally or less awkward.

I can't help but smile as Jess laughs along with me. She really is beautiful, and her laugh is so genuine it's impossible not to want to hear it again. She's got raven-black hair, the aforementioned most-beautiful-eyes-in-the-world, and a hard to place ethnic ambiguity. I start to think she's out of my league when I remember we don't even play the same sport.

"I'm so flattered," I say, "but I don't think I'm gay."

"And I'm not in the business of converting anyone," she says quickly. "I hope I'm not making you uncomfortable. Just to clarify, though, you don't *think* you're gay?"

"I mean, I'm not gay. I've never dated a woman. There was the occasional dalliance in college, but nothing serious."

"Well, then it sounds like we're on the new friends and free ice cream path." She laughs again. "I just fell in love with your idea of taking the year to really do some searching on this whole marriage idea. I'm not dating a new person every month, but I decided to give it a try myself."

"And how's it going?" I'm flattered that I've inspired someone else.

"Well, it's off to a bumpy, but interesting start." She gestures between us. "Here I thought I might have someone to get to know all month, but now I'm thinking I'll have to figure something else out. But at the moment, I'm a bit torn between two people and I'm mostly just confused."

"You're confused?" I say with an empathic laugh. "I'm so lost I can barely remember why I started this whole thing in the first place."

I start to fill her in on the origin of the Plan and my original status with Carter, who then dropped a bomb on me to kick this whole thing off.

"Here I was thinking I'd never be anything more than a fuck buddy," I say, suddenly aware that the wine has kicked in, "while he's working up the nerve to ask for something more. I think, anyway. I'm still not sure if he was already hoping to be with me, or if just the thought of not being with me scared him into saying something. I'm not even sure it matters, but it feels like it should."

"Oh, it matters," Jess says. "It would be one thing if you had been his focus from the jump, but you can't beat yourself up if he didn't even realize it himself until it was almost too late. I will say one thing though: it takes a super confident man to send you out into the world to date a bunch of other dudes to make sure he's the one."

I hadn't thought about it that way, but she's absolutely right. I was thinking Carter's willingness to suffer through this whole year must mean he's not actually suffering or isn't 100 percent sure about me, but it could mean the exact opposite.

"And what about the other guys you've dated so far?" Jess asks after we order our entrees.

"Well, January was a whirlwind and so wonderful, but it turns out there is some side drama there and it's completely over. I found out the friend who set me up with him had feelings for him herself and I nearly lost her over the whole thing. Now I just hope they can work things out because they really would be great together."

It's my first time saying that out loud, but I hear myself and know it's true. It's a nice feeling of closure.

"I thought February would just be a fling, but there was a bit more of a connection than I thought," I continue. "Definitely not a soulmate, but a nice guy and we had some fun."

"I bet," she says, smiling. "I saw his picture on that Gossip A to Z site and even for someone who prefers V to P, he was one fine specimen."

I laugh and nod, leaning in. "And those pictures didn't even do him justice. One fine specimen indeed."

We both giggle like schoolgirls and I sigh a big, relaxing breath, happy to have someone to talk to about everything.

"March was a guy I had a crush on in high school," I say, keeping the story going. "He reached out saying he'd had a crush on me too, and I about died. Things were okay, but not great, and then it turned out he had me confused with someone else the whole time. So now he's with her and I wish them well."

"Yikes," she says. "But hey—that's nice of you to have brought them together."

"I'm pretty much that old matchmaker lady from *Fiddler on the Roof*." I'm now barely able to talk through belly laughs. "I keep setting my dates up with other people. Hell, even my February guy is getting a ton of action from the whole website thing."

"So, who are you going to set April up with?" she asks, bringing my laughter to an awkward stop.

"Well." I'm unsure where to begin. "Maybe me, actually. I mean, right now, I'm not sure if I'm supposed to be with him or Carter."

"Ahh. So, that's your love triangle. Tell me about him."

I launch into the whole last month, beginning at the end of March with my spontaneous Disneyland trip with Eric, and Jess smiles as I talk, likely mirroring my face as I recount everything that's gone on in the past thirty-three days. I tell her how smart, kind, funny, and sexy my scientist guy is, avoiding the whole mermaid-in-the-lab thing.

"So how did it end?" she says, as I trail off thinking about how great Eric is.

"Well, it didn't technically. He is heading back to London as we speak to get a few things in order, then coming back here in two weeks to see if I'll leave Arizona and move there with him."

"Whaaaaaat?" Jess is taken aback at just the right level for news of this magnitude.

"Yeah, he got a grant and one of the requirements is that he does the work in London. I assumed that was it for us, but he asked me if I'd move there with him. He says he's in love with me. This all literally came out last night and I'm super lost. I actually came out tonight assuming I'd be telling some guy I can't date him because I need to get my head straight."

"Then I showed up and threw another wrench in the works and OMG no wonder you looked like you might faint on me when we met," she says, piecing everything together.

"Exactly. Is that similar to your situation at all?"

"Ha!" she exclaims. "Uh, no. Nothing that dramatic. I basically rekindled things with an ex to see if there's anything there, but also met another really great woman who I'm super excited about. And now I'm sitting across from you and wishing we hadn't actually met because before tonight, I could just pretend you weren't fantastic. But you are."

I blush and hope the lights aren't too bright in here.

"These girls in college," she says, leaning in again so that the people at the other tables don't hear. "How many were there and what all did you do? Any chance that was more than just experimentation?"

We're interrupted by our waiter who is dropping off our food and I'm very thankful for the distraction. It is hard enough to sort out my mind at the moment with two men but add a potential "am I actually bisexual?" crisis into the mix and my head might explode.

I mean, truthfully, I am pretty solidly in the middle of the sexual orientation spectrum. I knew growing up and I know now that I'm equally attracted to men and women, but just tend to prefer being with men. It's not so strong of a preference that I've ever completely eliminated the thought of dating a woman, but as I've been mostly focused on my career post-college, I've barely dated anyone other than Carter. Having to flirt with people from both genders just felt overwhelming, so I tucked it into the back of my mind, and there it has stayed.

Until now.

Chapter Fourteen

May 2

"So, technically, I wouldn't be breaking my promise to Eric by dating Jess," I say to Kim and Meg, trying to wipe the looks off their faces. "As a scientist, I think he would understand. I said I wouldn't date any men. Jessamyn is clearly a woman. Ipso facto, I am well within my rights."

"Are you in some sort of invisible court of law that we can't see?" asks Kim. "You do realize you're not on trial, right?"

"But if you were," says Meg, "I feel like we would definitely be finding you guilty."

We all laugh and take a minute to reach around the table for a taste of one of the many appetizers I ordered in my frenzy to eat my feelings while I sort this all out with my friends.

"You knew what he meant when he said that," Kim says, continuing the State's case against me. "You're supposed to be taking this time to decide between him and Carter. Or Arizona and London. Or just figuring out how you feel about Eric in general."

She's right and I know it, but I'm not kicking myself for agreeing to such limiting terms. If Eric were anything like Carter, he'd want me to be completely sure about him. And right now, that might mean ruling out women. Or, more accurately, woman.

"So how did you end things with Jess last night?" asks Meg.

"I told her I'd think about everything and call her soon," I say. "She seemed fine with that, and we chatted a bit more to get to know each other, then I paid for dinner and we parted ways."

"Did you kiss her?" asks Kim.

"On the cheek," I say. "It was all very respectful."

"Well, aren't you a good little lesbian," Meg laughs. "Your first date with a woman and you don't even try to get to first base."

"Trust me, it crossed my mind," I say. "She's beautiful and smart and funny. And she loves *Gilmore Girls*."

"So do we," says Kim, pointing between her and Meg. "But you've never once tried anything with either of us!"

Now we're all laughing again, and I decide to turn my attention to the food and drink taking up every available inch on our table. So much for simplifying my life to find some clarity. I need to talk to Kim and Meg about Eric, but so far, we've only talked about Jess.

"Okay," I say, after finishing a bite of southwestern egg roll. "Bisexuality aside, what am I going to do about Eric? How can I leave my home? What if I go there, realize we're not a good fit, and then I've uprooted everything for nothing?"

"Or," Meg says, gently, "what if you get there and it's everything you ever dreamed it would be? Don't get me wrong, I'd miss you like crazy, but when you started this whole thing you were looking for love. And then you fell in love. Maybe we shouldn't overthink it."

"But her friends, family, and job are all here!" says Kim. "How can she give that all up for someone she's only known for a month? Staying here was never even on his radar. It's just like the end of *The Little Mermaid*. Why does she have to get legs when her dad could have set him up with some fins?"

I laugh at the comparison, but she's right. Ariel wanted to live on land though, so maybe it's not a perfect analogy. Well, that and the fact she's animated. And fictional.

"That's true," says Meg. "Did you ask if there's any way he could or would stay here? Or come back here after a while? You love Arizona. And your house in California. That's a lot of concession for someone without the guarantee of a proposal."

"You guys are doing a great job of saying everything out loud that has been going through my mind," I say. "So, if one of you could just make a decision and tell me what I should do, that would be great. I know you think I'm kidding, but I'm not sure there's a wrong answer here. Maybe I should just flip a coin."

"Or maybe," says Kim, reaching across the table to put her hand on mine, "you should do what you told Eric you would and just think it through. Get out to San Diego this week and clear your head, then make one of those famous Rory Gilmore pro/con lists."

The image of sitting in my favorite beach chair while listening to the waves comes rushing to mind and I know she's exactly right. I can't think here, and I don't trust myself to not call Jess. It wouldn't be fair to involve her in all this anyway. She's got enough to think about on her own without combining our collective drama into one messy mess.

"You're right," I say, pushing back from the table. "Ladies, the ocean is calling, and I must go."

"Now?" my bewildered friends say in unison.

"Right now," I say, dropping enough cash on the table to cover the bill, tip, and maybe a little of my guilt.

I turn around and leave before either of them can say anything else, then turn back, realizing this is more dramatic an exit than I need to make. I go back to the table, hug them both, then walk away, get in my car, and head west.

Chapter Fifteen

May 3

I pull into the dark alley behind my house just after one in the morning, bleary-eyed but still happy with my decision. It's eerily quiet in the garage, but I can hear the water crashing on the sand as soon as I walk back out to my door. The moon tonight is bright, and I smile to myself as I turn toward the beach with sudden inspiration. If I can just run out to put my feet in the water for a minute, I know I'll fall right asleep.

As I'm crossing the sidewalk to hop over the wall onto the beach, I see a couple of teenagers eyeing me strangely as they kick a hacky sack back and forth under a streetlight. I could just keep going, but I don't really want an audience for my symbolic ocean-cleansing, so I just sit on the wall for a minute, contemplating my next move.

Then I smell what can only be pot and get hit with my second round of inspiration.

"Weed?" I say to the boys. "Do you have weed?"

I have never, ever in my life bought marijuana, but it suddenly seems like the best idea ever. I have tried it before at parties but have never been the one to procure it. I'm sure these kids can tell I'm a novice, but there's no one around and I'm feeling brave and reckless after my spontaneous drive.

"Uh, yeah," says the taller of the boys. "Twenty bucks."

I have no idea if this is the going rate for marijuana, nor how much he's going to give me for that price, but as it's an illegal transaction, I don't feel the need to ask too many questions. I find a twenty-dollar bill in my pocket, walk over, and hand it to him. In return, he hands me a baggie that looks to have a few joints in it, and they walk away.

Alone and now in the possession of drugs in public, I hesitate and consider running back into my house to hide. I look quickly to my right and left. Seeing no one, I decide to keep going and touch the ocean, damnit. I'm wearing a dress and sandals, so it won't even be that hard. I kick off my shoes and let the cold sand cover my feet for a second before picking up my shoes and continuing toward the water.

As I reach the spot where the tide is touching the shore, I am freezing. Or maybe I'm shaking with adrenaline. Hard to tell at this moment, but my feet are in the water and I close my eyes, waiting for the ancient healing powers of the sea to cleanse me of my confusion. Surely, a voice will come to me here to tell me what to do.

"Ever see *Jaws*?"

The ocean sounds different than I thought it would, until I realize the voice is coming from behind me and not from the Pacific I'm facing. I spin around to see an old man in his pajamas, smiling kindly at me.

"Cuz if you've seen *Jaws*," he continues, "you'd be too afraid to go out there any further."

He chuckles to himself, and I laugh too, remembering the opening scene and the ill-fated nighttime swim.

"I'm not going all the way out," I say. "Just wanted to feel the water for a second. What are you doing out so late?"

"Time is relative," he says. "And when you're like me and don't have much of it left, you learn to follow your instincts. I couldn't sleep, so I was looking out the window and saw you walk by. Given the choice between seeing a beautiful woman from far away or going up to say hello, I went with the latter."

"That's sweet," I say, and I mean it. "I just drove out here to clear my head. I didn't even pack before getting in my car. I guess I followed my instincts too."

"Ben," he says, by way of introduction.

"Cynthia," I reply, moving my shoes to my left hand so I can shake his.

"I hope you find some clarity here." He turns to walk away.

"So do I." I turn back to the ocean for one last look.

I walk back up to my house and let myself in. The other half of my house is rented out, so I'm careful not to make too much noise, but with no luggage and no extra guests, I think I manage to be relatively silent. I brush my feet off with one of the towels I leave by the door, open a window to let the sound of the ocean inside, take off my dress, and climb into bed.

"Here's to following instincts," I think to myself as I drift off to sleep.

*

I'm not sure how long the sun has been up when I wake in the morning, but my room is bright and breezy. I must have slept in, because mornings are normally a bit gloomy here with the marine layer. I reach over to check my phone and gasp aloud as I read the number 11:11 on the screen. I haven't slept in this late since I was a teenager, but I guess I was more exhausted than I realized.

In the spirit of following instincts, I get up, find some clothes in the closet to throw on, and leave in search of food. The beach is dotted with groups and singles out to enjoy the beautiful day, but it's not nearly as crowded as it will be once school is out in Arizona, then California. I walk around the corner to a little Mexican restaurant where I know I can get a good breakfast burrito, but remember I've probably slept through their breakfast hours.

I manage to sweet-talk the kid who works there into making me one anyway and leave him a big tip to say thanks before sitting down to wait for my food. I look around the restaurant and realize I'm looking for Ben. Maybe it's his age, or maybe it's because he somehow managed to be wise in pajamas, but he could be a big help on this journey. He's not here, but I know he must be around this area if he saw me walk by last night. I'll just have to keep my eyes peeled.

I take my burrito to go and head back to my house where I eat it on the patio, breathing in the sunshine and salty air. This is exactly what I needed. I start to open my mind to the names and thoughts I've been working on clearing from it, but immediately feel too overwhelmed. Then I remember the pot I purchased last night.

I walk inside and find the little baggy still tucked into my crossbody purse. I momentarily worry that they sold me something more dangerous than weed, but it looks just like the joints I've smoked before and something they were thinking of smoking themselves, so it's probably fine. I honestly can't believe how chill I'm being about all of this, but I guess I'm too emotionally exhausted to stress over any other decisions. I light up one of the joints and inhale.

It burns and tastes terrible, but I'm committed and smoke the whole thing. Just like when I stood in the ocean last night, I expect some sort of epiphany to hit me immediately, but I guess that's not how it works. I feel no more enlightened than I did a minute ago…except wait a minute.

The world slows down and my thoughts start to swirl. I walk back out onto my patio to gaze at the ocean because that is the absolute right thing to do at this moment. It looks incredible. How did I get so lucky? I have two awesome guys and this whole ocean all to myself and life is just so beautiful.

Shit. I forgot that I sometimes get emotional when I'm high. But isn't emotion just the most beautiful thing in the world? Fuck yeah, it is. I get to be here on this perfect day while the rest of the world has to go to work and damnit why is everything so unfair? I should donate some money to people who have it not fair. They need it to be fair.

I'm rambling the thoughts of a high person and half my brain knows it, but the other half of my brain is telling it to just chill the fuck out and go with it. That half of my brain swears a lot, but damnit, I don't care. Look at the sun shining. The sun doesn't care if I say fuck. Or even just think fuck.

"Fuck," I say out loud.

I look up at the sun. Just as I suspected, it does not care. It just keeps shining on me because it loves me and it wants me to be happy.

"Thank you, oh glorious sun," I say out loud again.

The sun shines its approval. The ocean is even reflecting some light from the sun for me to see it again, so I'm pretty sure I'm the luckiest person in the world right now.

Cuz here's the thing. I love Carter. I loved him way before he said he loved me, but the thought of losing him was too scary. I was just fucking scared. He loves me and he's going to be a doctor. He fucking saves lives. Maybe he'll save my life one day. Holy shit, maybe he'll save our *kids'* lives one day. I should definitely marry a doctor. We'd have really awesome kids.

But shit, I love Eric too. I think. Can you love someone after a month? *Yes!* Ah—I'm yelling in my head. Calm the fuck down, brain.

But yeah, I love Eric. If I'd met him before Carter—psh, game over, man. It would be Eric and me and all the Disney fantasies I've always wanted would totally come true.

There's no Disneyland in London, but I bet he'd take me to Paris. I bet on like a Tuesday he'd just wake me up and be like "let's go to Paris," and I'd be like, "I love you."

It's so romantic that he wants to take me to Paris. That's where I want to be proposed to. I'm pretty sure I mentioned that to both Eric and Carter, but I'd better be sure. I get out my phone to send out that very urgent message.

Me: *Just fyi, I want to be proposed to in Paris.*

I send it separately to Carter and Eric because manners. It would be rude to send that as a group text. And I'm not rude.

I think I like to have sex with Eric and Carter the same. I think it's the same amount of like in the bedroom. I really wish one of them were here right now to have sex with me. I think I'm good at the sex and we should be having it now.

Stop thinking about sex, my brain is saying to my brain. *If you like having sex with both of them the same, this isn't something to be thinking about right now. It's a tie.*

But you know who might be really good at sex with me and I'm not sure how I feel about it? Jess. She's so hot and I think she'd make me feel really good. I remember sleeping with those girls back in college. It wasn't just fun. They were girls so they knew what girls liked. They made me feel really good. Jess should know that I think she'd make me feel really good.

> **Me:** *I think we'd have really great sex. I just wanted you to know.*

I smile, imagining her reading that text. I probably just made her day. Just made her fucking day. I'm so nice. My phone is buzzing in my hand and I'm not sure who it is, so I look down.

> **Carter:** *Noted.*

Well, good. He has made a note to propose to me in Paris someday. I hope he keeps that note safe so he can consult it before he proposes. I would say yes to him anywhere, but to be proposed to in Paris would just be so...ugh. I mean, so great. Now my phone is buzzing again.

> **Jess:** *I think we would too. Where are you?*

> **Me:** *I am in San Diego. Came here to clear my mind and I'm high right now, so it's pretty clear. But I was thinking of you so I thought you should know.*

Again, made her day. Who doesn't want to be told that someone is thinking of them? No one, that's who. I bet Jess is sitting at work like "Cynthia is thinking of me and that makes me so happy."

"Aww," I say out loud, picturing her doing just that. It's so sweet.

Jess: I could meet you there tomorrow if you like. What hotel are you at?

"Awww," I say out loud again, drawing it out longer this time because she's so cute. She thinks I'm at a hotel. Bitch, I have a motherfucking house here. I don't need a hotel. I come whenever I want.

Me: Not a hotel. I have a beach house. I rent it out on Airbnb, but I leave half of it open for me.

I snap a selfie with the house behind me and send it to Jess so she can see what I mean. Sometimes it's hard to understand in a text and she should see this pretty house.

Jess: Love it! That sounds perfect.

It is perfect. It's so perfect and I'm so glad Jess knows that. She's so awesome. I have the most awesome people in my life. Kim said I should come here and I did come here and now I can make all the right decisions because instincts and the ocean and old men and pajamas and weed. I have found the magic formula.

My phone buzzes again and I just know it's something awesome before I even look down. That's how great my life is.

> *Eric: Does that mean you're coming to London? It's just a short train ride to Paris, my love.*

See. I knew it would be awesome. I'm not sure if I should go to London, but if I decide to, Eric will take me to Paris and ask me to marry him and the whole world will be awesome forever.

But then I won't be able to see my ocean and this sun whenever I want to. Isn't London super rainy and cloudy all the time? That would make me sad. That is not awesome. Fuck, I have got to think this through.

A big cloud just came and blocked the sun, giving me a preview of London, I bet.

"I see what you're doing," I say to the sun. Or maybe to the cloud. I can't really tell who is at fault here.

> *Me: Not sure yet. How many days of sunshine does London have every year?*

That's the question I should have been asking all along. Eric is a scientist, and this is a science question. He will completely understand why I am asking. This answer might be the key.

> *Eric: Not sure, love, but not as many as Arizona, that's for sure.*

Duh. I knew that, Eric. Honestly, which one of us is the scientist here? I don't want him to hear how annoyed I am though.

> *Me: Ha-ha. Let me know when you find out the number. I would miss*

the sun.

And it's so true. The sun and I have bonded. Not just today, but every day, man. We have a thing, the sun and me. Sometimes, I wear sunscreen. Okay, every day I wear sunscreen, but it's not because I don't love the sun or take it for granted. It's because I know too much sun can give you cancer or bad skin and that's not a healthy relationship.

"But I still love you," I tell the sun.

The cloud moves out of the way and the sun is back to say it loves me too. I totally get it.

Everything is awesome.

*

I wake up in the Adirondack chair on my deck three hours later, confused about what time it is for the second time today. The phone on my lap tells me I must have fallen asleep out here, which makes sense. Other than making me emotional and chatty, I forget that weed also makes me sleepy.

My stomach rumbles and I remember that it also makes me super hungry. I do a quick check and am very thankful I'm wearing a hat and T-shirt with pants today. My little midday nap has earned me a bit of a sunburn, but it's only on my arms where the sleeves didn't reach. That could have been a lot worse. I'm remembering some thoughts about the sun and abusive relationships, but it's all a bit of a blur.

I stop by another local restaurant and order a salad to go. There are flyers up on the wall advertising this week's events, so I peruse them as I wait for my food.

"Ever see *When Harry Met Sally…*?" says a voice behind me.

"Ben!" I say, turning around. He's not in pajamas today but looks sporty in his board shorts and an Endless Summer shirt.

"Cuz if you've seen that movie, you know that two people who keep bumping into each other are destined to be friends," he continues his thought.

"I have seen it." I smile. "It's one of my favorites. But I think the whole point of that is men and women can't ever actually be friends. They do fall in love, after all."

"Well, if you insist." He takes my hand and kisses it. "I'm not worried about the forty-year age difference if you're not.

"Ben, I think this is the beginning of a beautiful friendship."

"And she quotes *Casablanca*." He mimes a knife to the heart. "Fine, friends it is. I was just on my way out anyway. So long, friend."

"Bye, Ben," I say, watching him leave.

My salad is ready, so I take it home to enjoy inside. The burn on my arms gets stronger as the day goes on and it's probably better if I don't make it worse by eating al fresco this time. My house smells faintly of weed and a bit of the buzz is still rattling around my head, but not nearly as strong as it was before.

I've only been up for a few hours today after sleeping in super late, but I'm still feeling pretty tired. I look at the bed and decide to climb back in it and watch a movie. I find *Jaws* on demand but fall asleep before the shark even gets a chance to kill his second victim.

I wake up after the sun goes down and walk outside to stretch and see what's happening this evening. The people who have rented my house have kids and they're using the patio to grill up some burgers and hot dogs. They catch me staring at them and look at me strangely for a minute, so I decide I'd better introduce myself. Besides, the burgers smell really good and I'm still in munchie-mode.

"I'm Cynthia," I say, walking through the gate and onto the deck. "I own the house."

"Oh," says the woman, clearly relaxing. "Nice to meet you. We're the Schmidts. We just love your house."

"It's our second year here," says Mr. Schmidt, offering his hand. "I'm Tom and this is Judy. And these are our kids. Can we offer you a burger?"

"I'd hate to intrude," I say.

"Don't be silly," says Judy, offering me a plate and nodding toward the grill. "Please, we insist."

Judy had better watch her back because Tom knows his way around that grill. The burger is the best I've ever eaten. Or maybe I'm still kinda high. Whatever, I love it and that dad bod of his has me in marriage-destruction mode.

I catch myself thinking these thoughts and realize I'd better get inside before I say something horribly inappropriate in front of the kids. The weed certainly relaxed me, and I probably did some good thinking at some point today, but I can barely remember it. I excuse myself, thanking them for the food and wishing them a wonderful week here, then scurry back inside before I can fantasize further about Tom and his magical grilling prowess.

I climb back in bed and turn the TV on, but soon decide I'll just let myself drift back off to sleep. I need to do some serious thinking out here, and I'm not sure I can do it high. I think I'll face the day sober and well-rested and see what brilliant thoughts come to me. Assuming I didn't kill off all my best brain cells today, that is.

Chapter Sixteen

May 4

It's not terribly bright when I wake up this morning, but I think that means I've gotten back to a more grown-up schedule. I reach for my phone and give a sigh of relief when I see that it's 6:00 a.m.

"Much better," I say to myself.

My arms are a bit sore from the burn I picked up yesterday, but my head feels clear and I take this as a sign that I can get some things figured out today. I find the running shoes I leave at this house in the closet, throw on a sports bra and shorts, and step outside to stretch and start the day on the right foot.

The sidewalk is empty this morning other than other joggers and walkers, so I easily find my stride without worrying about tripping over bikes, strollers, and slow-moving tourists. I had almost forgotten how much I love an early morning run by the ocean, but breathing in the misty air soon brings me back to some of my happiest memories. Here, I am strong and capable. There's nothing I can't sort out today.

I'm not sure how far I run, but by the time I get back to my house, I'm drenched with sweat and out of breath. I take off my shoes and socks, set them on the deck, and walk toward the ocean for what I know is going to sting. Before I can change my mind, I run into the surf and let the cold water freeze and numb my skin. I scream a little as it hits my stomach, then dive under the next wave and gasp as I come up for air.

The shock of the water mixed with my racing heart makes me feel so alive, I could cry. And also, so cold I could cry for different reasons. I run back out of the water as best as I can and head back up to my house for a warm shower. It's like heaven and I'm thankful as the feeling comes back to my fingers and toes.

Clean and refreshed, I throw on some comfy clothes and sit at the table with a pen and notepad I found in my nightstand. Making two columns at the top of the page, I label one Eric and one Carter, then stare at it. I'm still staring at it when a knock at the door jars me from my concentration.

As I walk to the door, I try to think of what traits I even want to focus on for this list, not stopping to think at all about who might be here this morning. Even if I had thought about it, I still don't think I could have come up with the face that would greet me as I opened the door.

"Hi," says Jess, standing there with a suitcase behind her and a beach bag on her arm. "I wasn't sure which door was yours, but I guessed and here you are!"

I'm so surprised to see her that it takes me a moment to register her presence. That ends pretty abruptly though, as she crosses the threshold and plants a kiss right on my lips, leaving her luggage and bag outside. Whether I'm fully aware she's here or not, it's hard to deny that someone is most definitely kissing me right now. And it's a really great kiss.

I realize my surprised lips might not be engaging fully in the kiss, so I pull away for a second to take a breath, then put my hands in her hair to bring her back in for a better effort on my part.

"There you are," she says. "I know I didn't say what time I'd be here, but for a second you looked so surprised I thought I'd made a mistake."

She steps back to grab her things and I usher her inside and close the door behind her. I'm eager to grab my phone and figure out what in the hell she's talking about, but I can't do that with her standing here, so I decide to just play along.

"Sorry," I say, as she sits on the edge of my bed. "I was just lost in thought, I guess."

"Not a problem," she says, taking my hand. "I know this is a big deal for you, so we'll take our time."

What in the hell is she talking about? How does she even know where I live?

"Do you need to use the bathroom or anything?" I ask, wondering if I can clear her from the room for long enough to read our texts.

"Actually, yes. I caught an early flight and practically drank my weight in water. Are you hungry? I could freshen up and maybe we could go get some breakfast?"

"Breakfast, yes." I latch on to the only thing that's made sense since I opened the door. "I'll change too."

"No, no. You look so comfortable. Let's just keep today chill and really get to know each other."

I look down at my oversized T-shirt and sweatpants and shrug, but she smiles and turns to use my bathroom. As soon as the door closes, I grab my phone and look back to see if I invited her here when I was high.

I see my embarrassing text about thinking we'd be good in bed together, but I definitely didn't invite her here. But then, I open the selfie I sent her and realize what happened. She said she'd love to be here with me, and I replied with a picture of myself and the house behind me. Clear as day just above my head is the hand-painted sign I made years ago with the address of the house and a nice beach scene. It really does look like an invitation. And I told her we should have sex.

I frantically put the notepad and pen back in the nightstand to hide all evidence that I am actually here to figure out the Eric/Carter situation and have just sat back down on the bed when Jess comes out wearing nothing but a bra, panties, and devilish look on her face.

"We're pretty casual at the beach," I say, stalling for time, "but most places do require a bit more than underwear if you want to eat there."

"We'll get to that," she says, walking toward me.

I have never felt frumpier or more disheveled in my entire life. Here I am, sitting in pants with a hole in the crotch and a T-shirt that makes me look like a little kid. I have no makeup on and my hair isn't finished drying from my shower. I'm not even wearing the two articles of clothing that are currently all Jess has on. How is she still walking toward me?

"Hi," she says, now standing directly in front of me. She smells like coconut or something tropical and I can't help but sigh as I breathe it in. I'm about eye-level with her breasts and they are perfect and perky sitting in her black lace bra. Her panties match, because of course they do, and I look up to see her gorgeous eyes locked on mine.

The word instinct pops into my head and I let everything else go as I stand up to kiss her again. She even tastes amazing and I can't help myself from kissing her neck and shoulders, moving her hair out of the way to put my lips on every inch of her sand-colored skin.

She reaches down to grab my shirt and lifts it over my head, interrupting me from exploring her body momentarily. I'm now only wearing these stupid sweatpants, but at least the shirt is gone and I can press myself up against Jess's breasts with only her bra in the way. For now, anyway.

I kiss my way down her chest until I am kissing and licking the top of her breasts. They are smaller than mine, but perfect, and I reach my hands up to caress them as I go. Her bra has a front-opening clasp that I manage to pop open easily, allowing me to now press our completely naked breasts against each other. I'm immediately overwhelmed with a warm sensation between my legs.

As Jess and I kiss and revel in the feeling of our bodies so close, she reaches a hand down to touch me where I can now feel myself getting wet. She's teasing me and only touching me through my pants, but giggles as she discovers the hole and I soon feel one of her fingers touch me as she explores me a bit.

"I can take those off, you know," I say, pulling away from a kiss to whisper in her ear.

"You could," she says, as I hear the fabric tear a bit and feel another finger tickling me. "But I'm doing just fine."

I moan as she expertly finds and starts stimulating my clit. All my memories of sleeping with women come back to me as I remember just how good we are at this part. Something about knowing the anatomy of your partner and knowing exactly what feels good makes women infinitely better partners than men. Why did I ever go back to dating men?

Tired of being teased, I reach down to remove the pants, then lay down on the bed, fully naked. Jess joins me and lays next to me as we kiss and touch each other more. She's still fingering me inside and out and I can't help but arch my back as it starts to feel better and better. Seizing the opportunity, she begins kissing and licking my breasts as she keeps her hand busy between my legs.

Then, she moves her way down until her face is between my thighs and just goes to town on my whole area. Her tongue is strong and she knows exactly what to do with it. She brings me closer and closer to orgasm, then slows a bit, before ramping things up again until my whole body convulses with pleasure. I lay there for a minute until the shaking stops, and smile as Jess comes back up and puts her head on the pillow next to mine. She's smiling at me and I realize I'm up to bat.

I reach my hand between her legs and inside her panties and try to do everything she did. I'm a bit rusty, but I'm pretty sure I remember how this all works. Besides, I know what feels good to me, so this should be a piece of cake. Jess looks into it, but not nearly as much as she did when she was working on me, so I decide to kick things up a notch and stick one of my fingers into her pussy, which I find warm and welcoming.

I use my thumb to reach up and stroke her clit, but can't quite get the rhythm right and now I'm wondering if my nails are too long and is this hurting her?

I keep going with my hands and decide to add some oral stimulation to the mix, focusing on her breasts. This seems to be better, and her body responds more as her nipples become erect under my tongue.

"Harder," she says, so I increase the velocity with which I am fingering her. "Not there," she moans, and I realize she's definitely more into the breast action. Not a problem, as this is my favorite part.

Using both of my hands and mouth, I pinch, pull, and lick all around both her breasts until they look a little red and sore. She's nodding and breathing heavier, so I get my confidence back and decide to head south. And that's where I run into trouble. As much as I am turned on by other women and can hang with 90 percent of this whole game, I have never been good at this part.

Sensing my hesitation, Jess lifts her head off the pillow and says, "Let's take a break."

"Really?" I say. "But I didn't get you off."

"I feel just fine. I know it's been years since you've been with a woman and I love that you've opened yourself up to it for me. We don't need to do everything right away. Besides, seeing you come for me was pretty damn hot. I'm more than fine."

"Should we get some breakfast?" I'm thankful that she's so understanding.

"That sounds great." She pulls me back up to her for a kiss. "And don't worry. I can teach you everything you need to know. We'll get there."

*

J ess and I are sitting on the beach in bikinis, taking turns telling stories from our lives and having a blast getting to know each other. I have a nagging feeling in the back of my head that I've just completely cheated on Eric, but if any of this gets me closer to clarity, I can only hope he'll understand.

"So, you were high when you texted me yesterday?" she says with a throaty laugh. "No wonder you were so bold."

"Yeah, I didn't even realize I had invited you here," I say. "But I'm so glad you came."

"No wonder you looked so surprised. I feel so silly now."

"No, no." I turn to face her. "The weed just relaxed me enough to say what I was really thinking. And trust me—you have nothing to feel silly about. I love that you were so spontaneous and willing to come here."

"We should smoke together and try fucking again." She lowers her voice. "Not right now or anything, but I bet you'd be an even better student if your inhibitions are gone."

I nod. "But what about you? You're already so good at everything. What happens when your inhibitions are lowered?"

"Oh honey," she says. "You ain't seen nothing yet."

We both laugh and go on with our conversation. Since we're already in that frame of mind, I decide to treat Jess like I have the other guys this year and ask her my infamous questions to see if we're compatible outside of the bedroom.

1. Given the choice of anyone in the world, whom would you want as a dinner guest? ("George and Amal Clooney," says Jess with zero hesitation. Jess is very committed to human rights and is one of the few people I've ever met who had heard of Amal before she married George. I shamefully realize I would want them to be my dinner guest for very different and very shallow reasons, but I love seeing them through her eyes. And it's not like I don't also admire all the good they do in the world. This question has made me oddly internally defensive. My bad.)

2. Would you like to be famous? In what way? (Jess says she would so that she could use her platform and position to do good in the world. It's a great answer. She's pretty wonderful. "I do worry though," she says, "about all of the negative attention I'd receive. I can take people criticizing me just fine, but I tend to shoot my mouth off to idiots and bigots. I'd probably stick my feet in my mouth all the damn time.")

3. Before making a telephone call, do you ever rehearse what you are going to say? Why? ("No, but I've been known to make several drafts of text messages before sending them. Once you push send on a text, there's no coming back. The words are just out there." I nod and make a mental note to adopt this policy. She's so smart.)

4. What would constitute a "perfect" day for you? ("I'm pretty happy today," she says. "I love being by the water and being able to relax with good company. But in more general terms, I'd say a perfect day consists of a mix of productivity and relaxation. I like to feel as

though I've accomplished something each day, even if it's small." I ask her if we should get off our lazy butts and go do something, but apparently, she counts getting me off as her accomplishment for the day. Works for me.)

5. When did you last sing to yourself? To someone else? (Jess's sister had a baby last year and she loves singing lullabies to her. "I don't have a great voice," she says, "but the baby didn't seem to mind. I can't wait to sing to my own children one day.")

6. If you were able to live to the age of ninety and retain either the mind or body of a thirty-year-old for the last sixty years of your life, which would you want? (Jess chooses mind pretty quickly. "I love seeing women who age gracefully," she adds. "I'm not afraid to look older one day, but I'd be pretty devastated if my mind started to go. Or maybe I wouldn't know and it wouldn't matter? Eesh, that's scary. Next question please.")

7. Do you have a secret hunch about how you will die? ("Okay, this one is almost worse," she says. I give her the option to pass and we move on.)

8. Name three things you and your partner appear to have in common. ("Other than our physical similarities?" she says, motioning from my body to hers. It's true, now that I think of it. We both are about the same height and weight and as we've seen each other naked, the comparisons don't end there. "I'd have to say we're both kind, thoughtful, and funny. But seriously—we both have perfect boobs.")

9. For what in your life do you feel most grateful? ("The acceptance and love of my family," she says. "Coming out was a breeze. My parents have always been so supportive of me, and this was just an extension of that. I have friends who have been shunned from their families and friends. My heart aches for them.")

10. If you could change anything about the way you were raised, what would it be? (Coming off the last question, I assume she won't have an answer here, but she surprises me. "I had a lot of pressure put on me as a kid," she explains. "My parents are immigrants, so they wanted us to do really well to prove that we belonged or something. I'm thankful in some ways because I wouldn't be so successful without them pushing me, but it would have been nice to feel I could just be a kid, you know?")

11. Take four minutes and tell your partner your life story in as much detail as possible. ("Well, I was born and raised in Los Angeles," she begins. "We were pretty poor to start, but my dad was going to school while they both worked, and things got better when I was about ten. But before that, we really had to scrimp to make ends meet. Even after we were comfortable, they were really careful to make sure we didn't overspend because they didn't want us to backtrack. But they were still really generous to our family and friends. When people would move to the States, we'd bring over food and welcome them to the neighborhood. It was a big deal. Even on days when I know my mom was exhausted, she'd still find the time and energy.

"I rebelled a bit in high school when the pressure was too much but got my shit together as the years went on. I definitely had a few Jess Mariano years in there, hence my letter to you, but seeing what my parents did for me helped me get back on track. I went to school at UCLA on a scholarship, but I've been in Arizona for about three years now. I love it, but it's nice to be able to get to California to visit often, especially now that I'm an auntie.")

12. If you could wake up tomorrow having gained any one quality or ability, what would it be? ("Is it lame if I say flying?" she says with a laugh. "I am kinda impatient and would love to be able to just fly places as needed. Even getting here today was annoying because I had to wait for the plane to bring me. I've gone skydiving a few times and it's incredible. I just wish I didn't need the parachute.")

As we finish chatting, the sun begins to set, and Jess stands up from her chair to come sit between my legs. We look at out the ocean together, and I gently run my hand along her legs, stomach, arms, and neck as the colors in front of us become more vibrant.

A tear drops from my eyes and onto Jess's shoulder and I realize how safe and content I feel. I may not be sure about a lot of things right now, but I know in this moment, I am at peace.

Chapter Seventeen

www.flavorsofthemonth.bloggerific.com

I hope you're feeling adventurous this month, friends, because our new flavor is called Chaos Defined. I threw together several flavors you wouldn't think go together and combined them to make something that either makes me crazy or a genius. You make the call.

My little dating experiment is temporarily on hold while I think some things through, but I'll post updates here when I can. In the meantime, keep posting on social media about anyone you're seeing from our speed dating events! I can't wait to hear all about your love connections, since apparently mine are now public knowledge. Ha-ha. Really, I'm fine.

Have a great May!

May 6

I t's been a really great couple of days with Jess, but I can't quite calm the nagging feeling I have that I need to come clean with Eric. I've pulled out the pro/con list a few times when Jess has been in the shower or otherwise occupied, and it's pretty clear he's definitely still a contender, on paper at least. And what Jess and I are doing can definitely not be classified as platonic.

We spent yesterday bouncing from the beach to different restaurants and back, enjoying the local Cinco de Mayo festivities. We were drunk on margaritas, starting at about 11:00 a.m. and coasting all the way through until about midnight. There was a lot of giggling, kissing, and playful touching throughout the day, but we were both exhausted from the sun and tequila last night, so we passed out before my next lesson in pleasing a woman could continue.

But this morning, Jess has a look of determination on her face that has me pretty sure my time has come.

"Where's your stash?" she says, raising her eyebrows.

"Oh, you mean this?" I pull a joint from behind my ear. I had a feeling she'd want to try it today and I've always wanted to do that.

"Light it up!" she giggles.

I do as I'm told, and we pass the joint back and forth between us until it's gone. I get up to get myself some water, as my mouth and throat feel super dry, then come back to sit on the bed by Jess while we wait for it to kick in.

It doesn't take long before my brain and body both relax, but I can't tell if Jess is feeling it as she stares out of the window at the ocean. I move to sit behind her and wrap my arms and legs around her so as not to impede her view, in case she's right in the middle of some big, deep thoughts. I'd hate to harsh her buzz.

We're both wearing shorts and T-shirts, but no bras, and I get the sudden urge to reach my hands up under her shirt and damn if that's not the best idea I've ever had. I have boobs and they are awesome, but feeling hers makes me so happy I want to cry all of a sudden. She's still looking out the window, but my hands are totally distracting her, and she leans back into me as she utters a soft "mmm."

"I want you to tell me what to do to you," I say, and I really do. I'm no longer worried that I can't do this, but I know I need some guidance and damn it, I can do this.

"You're doing great so far," she says. Aww, she thinks I'm doing great. This is so nice.

I'm still behind her, but I reach one hand down to her shorts and wiggle it in between her skin and waistband, then down even further until I can feel her wetness. It's warm and awesome and I'm going to make her so happy. Just like when I texted her the other day. But not really because I don't think she had an orgasm from a text message.

"Like this," she says, putting her hand on top of mine and guiding me around to show me what she likes.

"Ohhh," I say, although I really can't tell what's so different about this and what I was doing the other day. But she's clearly liking this and didn't love what I did last time, so I keep going. I suddenly feel like I need a better angle, so I jump off the bed to face her. I pull her shirt off over her head and slide her shorts off too. Holy shit, she's naked and so hot and she wants to do sex with me. This is awesome.

Because she's naked and sitting on the bed, I get an idea.

"Lie back," I say, and she does.

Now I get down on my knees and position myself so that I'm face to pussy with Jess and I spread her legs a little wider. I don't know what I was so worried about. I remember the word instinct and bury my face into her, trying to imitate what she and a few talented men have done to me over the years. I know a lot of activity is usually a good thing, so I am really in there, licking and sucking everything that my mouth comes into contact with. I think I'm doing pretty good, but I lift my head up to see if Jess is into it.

But then I get kinda sad because I'm not sure she is all that into it. She's lying there and she's been responding, but something doesn't seem right. But wait—I have an idea.

"Wait, I have an idea," I say out loud because Jess cannot read my mind. I don't think.

I jump up and open the nightstand drawer where I have a few toys I've used over the years. I grab two of them and head back to where I was. Is this cheating? She's not saying it is, but she does laugh when she sees what I'm doing.

"Is this cheating?" I ask because again—not a mind reader.

"Not at all," she says. "Sometimes we have to get creative."

I am super creative and I'm excited that Jess likes that about me, so I turn on the vibrator I've brought over and press it to her clit. It has multiple settings, so I start on the lowest one, then turn it up a bit as I finger her. Now she's really responding and her hips start to move around.

"Mm-hmm," she says, encouragingly. "Just like that."

I have always been a student who responds to praise, so I keep doing exactly what I'm doing, turning the vibrator up one more time and waiting for Jess to climax. When she does, it's so exciting I accidentally drop everything and clap. Because yay me.

I climb up onto the bed and kiss her as she comes down from the orgasm—the one I gave her, by the way. She's smiling a satisfied smile and so am I. Before I can ask for feedback because that's the kind of student I am, she gets up off the bed and grabs the toys I dropped on the ground. I move myself further up onto the bed and she crawls up after me.

"Your turn," she says. "And these are great, by the way, but when we're back in Arizona, I have some more fun ones we can use."

I smile because yay toys and yay this fine ass woman is now going to do sex things to me. I'm a little embarrassed that I needed help to get her off, but I'm quickly distracted because she's now taking off my clothes and here we go.

Jess works her way over my body and everything feels electric and amazing, but I'm also super chill. Now I'm almost panicking though, because what if I'm too chill and I can't come? She's going to be so disappointed except she just put my vibrator on my clit and holy hell this won't be a problem at all. I was nice and started it on the lowest setting, but Jess is holding it steady on me and it's shaking like crazy. I almost feel like I can't take it anymore when she puts the dildo I got out to use on her in her mouth. Once she gets it nice and wet, she slides it slowly inside me.

Oh, my goodness, my body is on fire and Jess is just fanning the flames. She moves the fake dick in and around, again knowing exactly what will feel good and just when I think life can't get any better, the orgasm of a lifetime quakes through me as Jess moves all the toys out of the way and brings her face down between my legs to get a front row view of the epicenter, I suppose. She's kissing and nuzzling me as I slowly stop shaking, then comes up to kiss me.

"Are you crying?" she asks. It's a weird question because I am so happy but holy moly there are tears on my cheeks and when did that start?

"Uh," I say, bringing my hands to my face to wipe the not-small number of tears away. "Apparently? But I think they're just happy tears. Or orgasm tears? Is that a thing?"

"I think that could be a thing," she says, lying down next to me.

We've both been taken care of and I'm hoping weed has the same effect on Jess as it does on me because I can feel myself fading. I hear her breathing start to slow and that's the last thing I'm aware of before dozing off.

*

If that last thing I was conscious of pre-nap was Jess's breathing, the first thing I'm aware of post-nap is that I can't hear her breathing anymore. I turn to the side where she was sleeping but find that part of the bed empty. I roll back the other way and see Jess, wearing her shirt and shorts again, sitting at the table and looking down.

"Whatcha doing?" I say, stretching and giving a little yawn.

"Reading," she says, stiffly.

I sit up, immediately aware of the tone shift that has taken place while I slept. I can see now that she's looking down at a notepad with two distinct columns. I look to the drawer next to the bed. I must have left it open after pulling out the sex toys. She must have seen the notepad there.

Jess is aware of my love triangle predicament, so I'm not sure why she sounds perturbed, but there's only one way to know, so I ask.

"Is everything okay?" I get up and walk toward her, pulling on my clothes as I go.

"Well, I'm not sure," she says.

"That's my pro/con list between Eric and Carter." This is possibly the dumbest explanation I can give to something so obvious. "You know, like Rory Gilmore?"

"Yeah, I get what it is. But what I'm wondering is when you've been writing it. Because this looks like you've been working on it since I've been here."

"I have. I only have another week until Eric comes back, and I wanted to be sure I had some things figured out before then."

"Things, but not me?" She looks up at me. "Why does this list only have two names on it? Am I just a little distraction for you? Just a fling so you can cross women off your list for good?"

Oh shit. I now completely understand how this looks. And whether I did it subconsciously or not, she's totally right. I haven't been factoring her into this decision at all.

"No, it's not like that," I start, but she's talking over me before I can explain.

"I thought this was my month with you. I thought you were going to give me a chance. I know you told Eric initially you wouldn't date anyone for the time being, but I assumed you had talked with him about that when you invited me here. But I guess you didn't mean to invite me, so that was stupid of me to assume."

"Technically, he asked me not to date any men," I say, trying to break in, quickly wishing I hadn't.

"You knew what he meant! And now you're being dishonest and inconsiderate to both of us. We just met and you don't owe me anything, although this is a pretty shitty way to treat another human being. But you said you love him. If this is how you treat people you love, no wonder you're still single."

She's still sitting and her hands haven't moved, but it feels like I've been slapped across the face. But even still, I'm more shocked by the truth in her words than I am angry by how she's said it.

"I'm so sorry," I say. "You're absolutely right. I never meant to hurt you. I'm not sure what to say."

She gets up and begins throwing her clothes and toiletries into her suitcase, not even looking at me anymore. She's going to leave, and I can't even think of one good reason why she should stay.

"Do you want a ride to the airport?" I ask.

"I don't want anything from you," she says.

And with that, she grabs her bags, gives me one last look, and leaves.

Chapter Eighteen

Gossip A to Z

May 10

Ice Cream Queen Heats Things Up With…a Woman?

Yes, that's right, friends. Apparently, Cynthia Blake is sinking to new levels of desperation. Just dating a ton of men wasn't enough for her, so she's switching teams. We caught Blake at a restaurant with a local lesbian attorney for what looked like an innocent evening. Maybe they're just friends?

But wait—a reader in San Diego spotted Blake and her new gal pal looking pretty cozy together on the beach in what can only be described as a romantic embrace. Has Ms. Blake already burned through the only men who would have her so fast she has to look to her own gender for love?

Nothing in Ms. Blake's blog posts mentions her being bisexual, so this is clearly a new revelation. Or has she been gay all along and just toying with these other men? I guess it's all a moot point anyway. If Cynthia Blake is so confused by this whole thing that she's willing to date literally anyone, we can say with confidence this is going to end badly for all parties.

May 12

Trying to hide out in San Diego may have started out as a good plan, but ever since the newest Gossip A to Z post went up, I can't help but look over my shoulder everywhere I go. How could I have been so stupid?

That question applies to quite a few things in my life right now. I still haven't heard from Jess since she left and don't think I will at all now she's had her face plastered all over the internet. I'm sure she's furious with me and she has every right to be. I know in my heart that I had/have feelings for her, but I obviously wasn't considering her in the same way I've been thinking of Eric and Carter. I am scum.

Adding more evidence to the scum idea is what this all means for Eric. I was planning to tell him about Jess when he gets back to Arizona in a few days, but with the pictures of Jess and me now all over multiple websites, I'm pretty sure he's aware. The first picture of us at dinner is really no big deal, other than it showing Jess's face really clearly. The second picture is less clear on who she is, but it's obviously me and we're all tangled up on the beach. I don't sit with friends like that and I'm pretty sure most straight women don't either.

I still feel safer here than I do back home, so I've decided to stay a few days after Jess left in another ill-fated attempt at clearing my head. I'm mostly just stress eating and binge-watching Netflix, but when I can get myself up and outside, I'm at least relatively comforted by the presence of the ocean. The sun, however, is clearly judging me. I haven't seen it in five days. I get it. I don't deserve anything bright and joyful at the moment.

I have gone through about ten episodes of *Parks and Rec* today, which seems excessive, but also awesome because it's so great. But hey, I didn't buy a house so close to the beach so I could sit inside all day. Out into the world I must go.

I drag my chair out into the sand and try once again to think about where to go from here. The truth is that I might not actually have as many options as I previously thought I did. If Eric is as hurt about me dating someone while he was away as I imagine I would be in that situation, it's probably over there. So, then, do I still quit everything and tell Carter I want to be with him? Will he be hurt thinking he only won by default? Did he?

It's mostly cloudy today and a bit breezy, so I've got a hoodie on as I sit here and think, making it difficult for me to realize that I'm being approached by someone until he's right beside me.

"Ever see *The Wizard of Oz*?" I hear Ben say.

I smile as I turn to see him pulling up his own chair to sit beside me.

"Well of course I have," I say. "Hasn't everyone?"

"I suppose they have. But not everyone has been wandering around looking like Dorothy lately."

"So, does that make you the Scarecrow?"

"I like to think I have a brain," he says with a laugh. "And I definitely have a heart. All good on courage too. You've just been looking a bit lost these last few days and I couldn't help but think that you look like a girl trying to find her way home."

"Maybe you're the Wizard?" I nod. "And you're supposed to fly me away in a great big balloon."

"Ah, but isn't that the point? You've had the power to get yourself home all along. Maybe you don't have magic shoes, but I'm pretty sure you aren't stuck here, my dear."

"Maybe I'm not stuck, but I sure could use some advice."

I take Ben through the last five months as quickly as I can, trying to include all relevant details without boring him to death. He's a good listener though, and I can tell he's taking it all in.

"Sounds like you have some apologizing to do," he says when I finish. "And none of that texting crap people your age like to do. A real apology is delivered face to face while looking someone in the eye.

Make your penance and see who still wants you around after that. You sound like a woman tortured by too many good options. It's not the worst problem to have."

"It's not," I agree. "But what if I apologize and they all decide I'm not worth the hassle? This whole mess with the Gossip A to Z blog and other websites is a nightmare."

"The greater nightmare would be living your life so concerned by what other people say that you forget to fall in love, stay in love, and navigate all the obstacles of life together. You are not perfect and neither are they. The right person for you will love you even when you've fucked everything up."

I laugh, but really think for a minute about what he's saying. As quickly as I made the decision to drive out here at Kim's suggestion, I know immediately that I need to get in my car again to head back to Arizona.

"Ben," I say, standing and smiling down at him, "thank you for telling me exactly what I needed to hear. I'll keep an eye out for you when I come back, but it's time for me to go."

"Good girl," he says, standing up to shake my hand. "I'll see you around, kid."

And with that, I drag my chair back up to my house, grab my purse, and lock up before giving the ocean a long look goodbye. I'll miss it, but I know where I need to be right now and it's not here. It's good to get away from time to time, but there's no place like home.

Chapter Nineteen

May 15

Today is the day Eric gets back to Arizona and my heart is beating a mile a minute. We made plans for dinner, but I have no idea how I'll eat. I thought about asking him to come to my house instead, but I'm a bit of a chicken and hoping that meeting in public will lessen my chances of being yelled at. I mean, I can't picture Eric yelling at me, but I would kinda deserve it.

I show up at the restaurant fifteen minutes before we're supposed to meet, hoping to see him walk in. But, alas, my plan is foiled by my scientist guy who has already arrived before me. He looks as handsome as I remember, and I momentarily forget that I've ever even been interested in anyone else as he crosses the room to hug me.

"Welcome back, world traveler," I say into his shoulder. This hug is lasting forever, but I don't care. Eric kisses the top of my head and I let myself melt into his arms a little deeper.

"Hi," he says, pulling back for a moment to look at me. There's a sadness in his eyes as he takes me in, and my stomach lurches as two words cross my mind. *He knows.*

"Shall we?" he says, motioning to the hostess who has come to tell us our table is ready. "After you."

We walk through the restaurant and I'm convinced that everyone is looking at us, just waiting for him to scream and cry and call me a horrible person. I know it's all in my head, but it's hard to get a hold on reality with such a devastating conversation looming.

As we sit down, I decide to go for the old ripping-off-the-Band-Aid approach.

"There's something I have to tell you," I say, confused that I'm hearing it in stereo. Apparently, Eric said the exact same thing.

"You go first," we both say together, our manners and like-mindedness making it tough to communicate at the moment.

"I'll go," he says, and I'm grateful for the chance to hear him out before figuring out what I'm going to say. "When I left, I told you I wanted you to take some time to think things through. And even though I thought I had everything figured out on my end, being home brought out a few things I hadn't considered. It was wrong of me to just ask you to disrupt your life and move to be with me, when it had never crossed my mind that I could do the same for you."

I love his words, but they are making me feel even guiltier. I consider stopping him before I feel worse, but he goes on.

"I talked a lot with my family and friends, all of whom are dying to meet you, by the way," he says with a smile. "But while I was out at a pub with my mates one night, I ran into an old girlfriend who I haven't seen in years."

Hold on. This has taken an unexpected turn.

"Oh?" I say calmly but I'm wondering where the heck this is going.

"She and I broke up when I moved to the States. She moved on and so did I, obviously, but seeing her again got me all confused. We talked for hours, and both realized there are still some very strong feelings there. Nothing happened, but only because I didn't know where you and I stand. I'd be lying if I said I didn't want something to happen. I'm so sorry, Cynthia."

A wave of jealousy washes over me before I can even stop to think how hypocritical I'm being. Not only did I, also, meet with someone I have feelings for, but something *did* happen. And it wasn't even an ex who I had previously loved. That would have been a bit more forgivable. And here Eric is apologizing to me for just talking with someone. This is going to be harder than I thought.

"You really don't need to apologize," I say, watching Eric sigh in relief. "I have something to tell you as well."

"Did you see Carter while I was gone?" he asks.

"No, but there was someone else," I admit. "I hadn't had a chance to call off my May person after you left, so I showed up to our first date to break it off face to face. It felt rude to do it over the phone or text."

"Did you sleep with him?" Eric asks, looking hurt.

"It wasn't a him. Her name is Jess, short for Jessamyn."

"Ah," Eric laughs. "So, it was all a misunderstanding."

"It was," I say, hesitantly. If he's laughing this off as preposterous, this is about to get ugly.

"I was worried you were going to say you cheated on me. I know I don't have a high moral ground here after reconnecting with an ex, but I'd still be hurt, I guess."

"Well, here's the thing. I had no intention of dating Jess, but I went to San Diego to clear my head and she was under the impression that I invited her there. It's a long story, but I was high and she just kinda showed up."

"You were high? I didn't realize you do that."

"I haven't in years," I say, defensively. "But I was so confused and I thought it would help clear my head. But anyway, she showed up. And, well, one thing led to another, and we had sex. Twice."

Eric is silently staring at me, but his poker face is incredible and I have no clue what he's thinking.

"Hang on," he says. "Allen sent me that Gossip A to Z post, but I just assumed it was one of your friends. Are you telling me you're gay?"

"No, no," I say. "I guess I'm bi, but I'm not even all that good at the whole girl thing. If I hadn't told you I wouldn't date anyone while you were gone, it would have made sense for me to fully date Jess. The whole point of this year was for me to figure out exactly what I want. And the truth is, I am attracted to women."

"I, uh, I'm a bit confused right now. I assumed I'd be the one with something to apologize for tonight, but this is all more than I was expecting to hear."

I grab Eric's hand and look him right in the eye.

"Eric, I am so sorry," I say. "I told myself that you said not to date any men, so a woman wouldn't technically be cheating, but that was wrong. In fact, it was wrong of me to make you that promise in the first place when I've been trying all this year to keep searching for my future spouse. I never meant to hurt you and I hope you can forgive me."

Our waiter is standing right by our table but seeing us in such an intimate conversation has rendered him speechless.

"We need a minute," I say to him.

"I need more than a minute," says Eric as he moves to stand. "I'm not mad. Or maybe I am. I don't know what I am. I'm sorry, Cynthia, but can we talk again tomorrow? I'm a little jet-lagged and this was a lot and I think I need some time to think."

"Of course." I stand up. "Go ahead. I'll give you a head start before I go."

He nods, turns, and leaves. And here I am, alone again after hurting someone I care about.

It's not a great track record.

Chapter Twenty

May 16

"Sorry to wake you, but there's something you need to see right away."

It's 6:00 a.m. and Sam is once again calling me to alert me of something. This cannot be good. Or maybe she's calling to say we just won the lottery. That would be weird, seeing as how we don't play, but it's too early for my brain to function and well, here we are.

"What do I need to see?" I say groggily.

"Jess posted an op-ed piece about you and it's all over social media," says Sam.

Shit. Shit shit shit. I barely slept, worried all night that I've ruined multiple lives, and now someone I've hurt has gone public with how shitty I am. I guess I had this coming.

"It's not what you're thinking," she says sympathetically. "But you need to see it. We're getting media requests like crazy. And not just local people."

I move my phone away from my face and click on the link Sam texted me while we've been talking. I tell Sam I'll call her back as the page loads.

Dating Cynthia Blake: The best/worst thing I've ever done

I am furious right now and need to set the record straight. First of all, let me state for the record that Cynthia Blake and I are not now, nor have we ever been, a couple. I first learned of Ms. Blake from an article about her search for love this year and was so intrigued that I reached out to her asking for a date. I did not tell her I was a woman, which lead to some pretty understandable confusion at our first meeting.

What happened next is between Ms. Blake and myself, or so I thought until I saw the nasty article written about us on the garbage website Gossip A to Z. First of all, where do you get off, judging Ms. Blake for allegedly dating a woman, as if bisexuality is some inherently terrible thing? This woman is trying to find someone to spend the rest of her life with. She should be exploring all avenues that feel right to her and shame on anyone who tries to judge her.

I know Cynthia to be a very kind, funny, and warm person.

Any person would be lucky to end up with her and she has a big decision on her plate this year. Following along with her journey can be a great learning experience for all single people, most of whom will never be so bold as to try what she's doing. I characterize my time with her as the best and worst decision because as much as I care for her, we are not meant to be. Getting to know her only made that harder to acknowledge because I know just how special she is.

The hurtful undertones of the Gossip A to Z post reek of homophobia and bigotry, not to mention slut-shaming and self-righteousness. I truly hope I never learn the identity of the writer of these posts. It would be hard for me to remain civil in the presence of such a hateful person.

tl;dr Cynthia Blake is awesome and whomever is attacking/stalking her sucks.

I finish reading and realize I have tears in my eyes. I know I hurt Jess, so for her to speak up defending me is just incredible. I need to see her soon to tell her how sorry I am and how much I appreciate her in person, but I call Sam back first to check in.

"Wow," I say. "What kind of media requests are we getting?"

"Lots of interview and comment requests. And one production company sent an email last night asking if you'd be interested in starring in a reality show."

"Hard pass," I laugh.

"To which one?"

"All of it, for now," I say. "I'll post on the blog soon, but I don't want this to turn into a media circus."

"No offense, Cyn, but it kinda already has," says Sam.

She's right and I know it, but I don't feel like adding fuel to the fire by going on the defensive.

"How are you holding up with all of this?" I ask, realizing this question is terribly overdue.

"Well, it's a bit overwhelming," she says. "And I'm worried about you. But I think I'm okay. I'll let you know if it gets to be too much."

"Please do. I'll talk to you later."

I was thinking I'd try to go back to sleep, but I'm wide awake now, so I get up to take a shower. On my way to the bathroom, I send Jess a quick note.

Me: Can I see you today? There is so much to say.

I hear my phone ping when I'm in the shower and come out to find her reply.

Jess: Of course. I agree. How about lunch?

I breathe a sigh of relief, and we make a plan to meet near her office in a few hours. In the meantime, I forward both the most recent Gossip

A to Z post and Jess's reply to Carter, just in case he hasn't seen them.

Carter: Sounds like you could use an escape for our month.

Me: OMG yes. Get me out of here.

Carter: Have your passport ready and bags packed. I've got it all worked out.

Well, heck, that sounds promising. I'm not supposed to see Eric until tonight, and I wonder for a minute if I should send him what Jess wrote. It doesn't change the fact that I slept with someone else when I was supposed to be figuring things with him out, but it does color things differently.

I look absentmindedly out of my window while I think about that, but as I'm convincing myself it's not a good idea, something strange catches my eye. There's a black SUV parked in a spot facing my condo, which is not unusual on its own. What's weird is that I can see someone sitting in the front seat with a long lens pointed up toward my bedroom.

After closing all the blinds and curtains in the house, I slump down a wall and start to cry. I knew I've been followed lately. It's the only thing that makes sense for the pictures that have been posted. But seeing someone outside my house, just waiting to see what I'll do… I could throw up.

Me: Black SUV outside my condo. Photographer sitting in the driver's seat. What do I do?

Kim: *You do nothing. I'm on my way.*

Me: *Please don't murder anyone.*

Kim: *No promises.*

Kim only lives a few minutes away, but I'm still surprised when I hear tires squealing so quickly. So much for sneaking up on the guy. I peek out of the side of the window to see Kim's car speeding toward the SUV, but he hears/sees her coming and is pulling away about as fast as she's coming in. My heart skips a beat as I think she might pursue him, but she comes to a stop and slams the steering wheel in frustration before she gets out and walks toward my door.

I meet her there with a hug before unleashing a few swear words.

"What were you thinking?" I ask. "You could have been in an accident!"

"I was just trying to get in quickly so I could get the license plate number and see his face before he got away," she says, shaking with adrenaline. "But I only got the first two letters and couldn't see his face at all. I'm so sorry, Cyn. At least he's gone."

"No need to apologize. I was just worried about you. Do you know what kind of car it was?"

"Black?" she offers. "Big?"

"Man," I laugh. "We suck at police work."

"Yeah, I guess we didn't really think this through. Are you okay?"

"I'm creeped out. But I'll be okay. Maybe I should call the actual police next time. Is this even illegal?"

Kim shrugs and we both collapse into chairs in my kitchen with fits of laughter. It's nice to laugh after feeling so upset just minutes ago.

I show Kim Jess's article and fill her in on my time in San Diego.

"Aww, I love this Jess person," she says. "Are you sure she's not the one? Maybe if she knew you were really considering her as an option, she might change her mind."

"I'm having lunch with her today to chat," I say, "but I think on some level I had already ruled her out before even giving her a chance. I was seeing her as a friend and I really care about her, but I looked at her also as a representation of all women. That wasn't fair."

"Yeah, I can see that. Sounds like she's too good for you anyway."

I throw a dish towel at Kim, which she deftly catches and tosses back at me. It's just the kind of levity I need after such a crazy morning. We chat for a while longer and Kim fills me in on what's been going on with her. School is almost over for the year, and she's been talking with Javier, but it's still a bit awkward.

"I think the summer will do us both some good," she says. "I feel like everyone is watching us at school."

"Tell me about it," I say.

"Oh, yeah, sorry." She sounds sheepish. "I guess you know what that's like."

I check my watch and realize it's just about time for me to meet

Jess, so Kim and I walk out together. We're both scanning the area for the black SUV or someone else with a camera. Seeing nothing, we take off in separate directions.

As I pull up to the restaurant where I'm supposed to meet Jess, I see her walking from her car to the entrance. She looks effortlessly beautiful in a simple sundress, and I feel ridiculous once again for ever thinking I could be in her league. Not only is she beautiful, but she has proven herself to have grace and class under fire. Once again, I feel like scum.

I take my scummy self into the restaurant and search the tables for her. She sees me and waves, smiling a smile I surely don't deserve. She doesn't stand up to hug me when I get there, but that seems more than fair.

"You didn't have to do that," I blurt out. "But I can never thank you enough."

"I did have to," she says. "Whoever is writing that garbage needs to be put on blast. They weren't just attacking you. There's some real deep-seeded nastiness there."

"Even still, I can't imagine how hard it must have been. I'm so sorry I hurt you. I'm sorry I didn't give you, give us, the respect I should have."

"Hey now. It's not like I came into this thing under fully noble pretenses. I told you when we met that I also had a couple people on the hook. I'm not sure I was ever fully invested in us either. I mean, I think you are wonderful, but I brought my past into our time together just like you did. Maybe I lashed out at you because I was projecting some of my own insecurities onto you."

"All I know is," I begin, "I will always be incredibly grateful that you came into my life. You really are the Jess to my Rory."

"Because I don't take your shit and see you for who you could be instead of who you are?"

"Exactly. And since you brought it up, who should I be?"

She laughs but takes a minute to choose her next words carefully.

"You should be unapologetic and bold," she says. "Do not let the judgment of others knock you off course this year. But you should also be vulnerable and curious. Let the people you are inviting into your life really come into your life. And don't call this whole thing off until you've seen it through until the end. Eric was wrong to ask you to do that. It says more about him than it does about you."

Now it's my turn to take a minute to choose my words. She's right. Carter knew me well enough to let me figure this out away from him. Maybe Eric just didn't have the confidence to do the same.

"I'm so sorry about the whole Gossip A to Z thing," I say. "Truly. You're going to get a lot of hate mail for your reply."

"I'm an outspoken lesbian who works with human rights cases," she says, looking me right in the eye. "I stand up for the voiceless in literal life or death situations. A trashy website is not going to be the thing that breaks me. And I won't let it be the thing that breaks you either."

"Are you sure we shouldn't be together? Cuz I'm really loving you right now."

"I think you're wonderful and I know we'll be great friends, but to be honest, you're terrible in bed."

I watch her face to see if she's kidding, then join her when she starts to laugh.

"I thought you were serious there for a minute," I say, relieved.

"Well," she says, "maybe not terrible, but I think you've been with men too long. Don't get me wrong—it would have been fun to teach you a few more things, but honestly, I just don't have the time."

We both crack up with laughter and spend the rest of the lunch chatting about much less serious things. I compliment her dress and she offers to take me shopping. We manage to avoid anything about my love life until she leaves me with some parting words on our way out the door.

"Watch your back, Cyn," she says, and the hairs on my arms stand up. "You should assume you are being followed everywhere. We both know the people behind this website are idiots, but they could still do some damage to your life and business."

"Yeah, my only laugh about all of it has been all of their stupid typos," I say, trying to lighten the mood.

"I find that angry people don't always have the best grasp on grammar," she agrees. "But seriously, I will always defend you, but this could get ugly."

I nod and walk to my car, unable to shake the feeling that she's absolutely right.

*

With how well my lunch with Jess went, I feel a bit better about meeting with Eric tonight. He's coming over to see me so we can chat and even though I know I owe him some very real apologies, I realize he might owe me a couple as well. I don't need him to by any means, but I feel slightly better knowing we both took some missteps.

When I hear a knock on my door, I yell for him to come in while I finish making dinner. I look over my shoulder to see Eric smiling at me and I'm even more relaxed. He looks ready to forgive me. Or maybe he just loves the sight of a woman cooking.

"You look beautiful even while you cook," he says.

"That's just your stomach talking," I say, finishing up and heading to the sink to wash my hands.

"I'm so sorry." He joins me at the sink. "It wasn't fair for me to judge you when I basically spent our whole time apart with someone I have feelings for. I never should have asked you to abandon your plan."

"But you did, and I agreed. So, I should have kept my word. I'm so sorry, Eric."

"So now what do we do?" he asks.

"We eat dinner," I say. "And maybe talk a bit, openly and honestly, about what we want."

And that's just what we do. I tell Eric about my pro/con list with him and Carter.

"How'd I do?" he asks.

"Just fine," I say. "The cons were mostly logistics. I'm just not sure I could move to London. Well, I'm sure I can't right now."

He nods, looking sad, but I know he understands. Just like it would have been hard for him to stay here long-term, it would be as tough for me to uproot my life for him when I'm not even halfway through the year.

"I'll give you the same space Carter did, then," he says, sounding resolute. "Let's see how we feel at the end of the year."

"Deal," I say. "Thank you for being so understanding."

"Must be my princely nature. We royals are known for our magnanimity."

"Pretty much every movie I've seen about the monarchy would suggest otherwise," I laugh.

"Well, we can't all be winners." He smiles.

"When are you heading back to London?"

"Tomorrow, actually. We've already been pretty busy in the lab and I keep getting angry messages from Allen about how I've abandoned him or something."

"Then I guess we should make tonight count." I stand up and walk toward my bedroom.

Eric, not being stupid and being very much male, jumps up to follow me and chases me down the hallway. We land on my bed in a heap and start kissing furiously. There's a different feel to our connection though, and I can't tell if it's because I'm sad that he's leaving or a bit unsure of why he came back in the first place.

I feel hot, wet tears on my face before I realize I'm crying. Eric seems emotional too.

"I felt so sure when we talked yesterday that I could leave you again easily," he says, pulling away from me. "But holding you again like this makes me want to tell Allen to piss off."

"I know what you mean," I say, swiping my fingers over my cheeks. "I can't put it into words on any list, but I feel it deep inside me. This is just so right."

"Speaking of feeling things deep inside you," he quips, breaking the tension. "Sorry, sorry—I had to say it."

I laugh and roll over on top of him where I feel exactly what he'd like to put deep inside me. We rock back and forth a few times, still completely clothed, then Eric rolls me over so that I'm on my back. We both do the awkward undressing thing where we're still kinda laying down next to each other, but it gets the job done and soon we're both naked, eager, and likely still emotional.

"I love you," he says, entering me slowly. I shed another few tears, realizing this is the first time we're having sex since saying those words to each other.

I want to say it back, but I instead pretend to be too caught up in the moment to speak. If I really loved him, wouldn't I have been willing to go to London for him? Love should be unconditional, and I feel like I've thrown the condition of only being able to love him if he stays here onto our fate. Does that negate how I feel? Can my heart really love two people at the same time?

I try to focus on Eric, who is very much focused on our lovemaking. And it does feel wonderful to be literally connected to him like this. I turn off my brain for a minute and just let myself enjoy the feeling of him. It's not our greatest time in bed, but he seems satisfied enough and I can't help but smile as he kisses me before getting out of bed.

We decide to curl up in bed together to watch a movie before falling asleep in each other's arms. I opt for *La La Land,* hoping the ending will be a subtle clue for him about how I feel, but Eric falls asleep before I can tell him cinematically what I know in my heart to be true.

That wasn't love we were making; that was saying goodbye.

Chapter Twenty-One

Gossip A to Z

May 29

So many of you have written in or commented on our social media page about Cynthia Blake's behavior this year, we feel it's time to speak out. After she ditched her lesbian-du-jour, we brought you the exclusive photos of her back with Mr. April later that day and frankly, it's just disgusting. Many of you have expressed outrage over a woman who owns a family-friendly business engaging in something so morally wrong.

In response, we've decided to take action. Starting today, we are calling for a boycott of all Sinfully Good ice cream stores. If you'd like to show your support, we'll also be picketing at different locations to let customers know what they're supporting if they continue to support Ms. Blake. Don't worry, readers. We'll show Ms. Blake she can no longer flout

the morals of society without any repercussions.

May 29

WELL, I'M PRETTY much in full panic mode, but luckily the protests aren't going all that well. I hate to leave Sam at a time like this, but I feel like I'm about to go crazy and she keeps assuring me she can handle it. She's quite a bit feistier than I am, so I have stopped texting her every hour. Instead, I'm packing to leave on my mystery-trip with Carter.

The timing could not be better, as I now can't leave the house without one or more cars following me. It's not just Gossip A to Z anymore, as some local and national outlets have become interested since the call to protest came out. It's almost a little better now that I can see them all, but it's also the worst feeling in the world and OMG when is Carter going to be here so we can leave?

Right on cue, I hear a knock at the door. I answer it to see him standing there with the biggest smile I have ever seen on his face.

"I've got two tickets to paradise," he sings badly, stepping inside to kiss me. "And you look like you could use a getaway, baby."

"You have no idea," I say. "So now are you going to tell me where we're going?"

"I suppose," he says with a devious smile. "Any interest in a

Tuscan villa, far away from the chaos and bullshit back here? Cuz if not, I will go without you."

All my life, I've dreamed of seeing the Italian countryside and Carter knows it. I am so happy I could cry. Oh wait, I am crying.

"Like hell you will," I say. "Let's get out of here."

How do you say holy fucking shit in Italian?

Chapter Twenty-Two

www.flavorsofthemonth.bloggerific.com

Ciao, friends! I am writing this month's only blog post from the airport on my way to Italy, where I fully intend to unplug, relax, and explore with this month's flavor. The flavor you all get to experience this month will be a mint chocolate chip gelato because it's my all-time favorite flavor, but with an Italian twist.

I want to thank all of you who have stayed loyal to our stores and, by extension, me through all this craziness. I am sure the protests will die down soon, especially as it heats up back home. I can't imagine anyone being angry enough with me that they'd be willing to spend hours outside when it's 110 degrees and there's delicious ice cream just feet away. I hope not, anyway. Our speed-dating events this month will take place at different locations, just in case, but we'll have plenty

of delicious, Sinfully Good ice cream on hand for you to enjoy

with your new potential dates. Until next month, arrivederci!

June 1

I am Audrey Hepburn in *Roman Holiday*. People are staring at me as we exit the plane in Rome because the resemblance is so uncanny. I may not resemble her physically, but it's the grace I carry myself with that has them hypnotized. I can just feel it. Sure, I've been on a plane for nine hours and I dozed for a bit, but the excitement of this trip and sharing it with Carter has me feeling like a new woman, who is not at all jet-lagged. I am rolling this suitcase like a movie star and deftly pull it onto this escalator with me so I can look out over the lower concourse and smile demurely at the throngs of people who have turned to look at me, Audrey 2.0.

Except, wait a minute. What are those posts at the bottom of this escalator doing there? Was that sign with a picture of luggage on the escalator with a big X and something written in Italian more than just a suggestion? What the fuck do I do now? I'm going to run into those posts and this thing isn't stopping and—

"Ack, *shit*, oof!" I exclaim, lifting my carry-on suitcase over the posts at the last second and nearly falling over as I scoot my body between them. I turn to see Carter easily turning his suitcase sideways and walking like a normal person between the posts, leaving plenty of time for the people behind him to do the same.

"I, uh, thought my bag wouldn't fit and panicked," I say, lamely.

"Yes, I see that," says Carter, not even trying to hide his laughter. "You all right now?"

"Who, me?" I say with mock confidence. "I'm Audrey Hepburn, baby."

"Guess that makes me Gregory Peck?" He gives me a proud smile. I made Carter watch *Roman Holiday* years ago and I am thrilled to hear he remembers it.

"Indeed, it does." I lean forward to give him a quick kiss. I'd kiss him longer, but we did a fair amount of that on the plane ride and there are still a few onlookers after the ruckus I made getting off the escalator. My cheeks blush as my brain flashes a few images from our journey, and I get the feeling Carter is on the same wavelength as I catch a sheepish smile.

It's not like we joined the mile high club or anything, although I was totally down for that. I've really missed Carter, so even if the plane had been bound for Des Moines (apologies to Iowa, but it ain't Italy), I'd have been about ready to jump his bones midair. But combine the whole absence-makes-the-heart-grow-hornier feeling and the prospect of Tuscany on the horizon?

"Meet me in the bathroom," I had said, in between passionate kisses in our seats.

"Uh, we haven't taken off yet," Carter had reminded me, laughing. "And I think we're going to have another person sitting here soon who probably won't appreciate our current situation."

Sure enough, a friendly, middle-aged woman sat down in the aisle seat next to me and began politely inquiring about our trip. She truly could not have been nicer, but I have little patience for cock blockers. Luckily, she fell asleep somewhere over the Atlantic, at which time I happily resumed making out with Carter, but we couldn't get nearly as freaky as I'd have liked in such a small space.

And thus, my head is spinning not only with exhaustion as we make our way through the airport, but also the intense desire to pull Carter into a family-size bathroom and rip his clothes off. He sees me eyeing one as we pass and gives me a "don't even think about it" look before I can say anything.

"Trust me," he says. "You're going to be happy we waited when you see where we are headed."

"Are we staying the night in Rome?" I ask, flushing with excitement of the tourist variety.

"Not tonight. But we'll come back here before we leave. I just thought some time in the Italian countryside might do us both some good to start."

"You sure I can't talk you into a quickie in one of those *baños* over there?" I raise my eyebrows.

"Cyyyyyynnnnnnn…" Carter drags out my name. "You're not

going to do that thing you do where you are around foreign people and just start blurting out Spanish words, are you?"

"Maaaaaaaaayyyyyyyyybbbbbbbbbeeeeee," I say, then crack up with laughter. I speak some Spanish, but Carter is referring to my tendency, on many occasions, to use it at really wrong times. Like when greeting people from France at my store. Something in my brain just goes haywire and sends a signal telling me to say any foreign word I can think of. The results have varied from silly to downright cringeworthy, like when I famously tripped in an Oslo restaurant years ago and shouted, "*Hola!*" I was trying to let people know I was okay, and instead convinced them of the opposite.

We laugh and chat the rest of the way through the airport, and I watch with awe as Carter navigates us to the rental car counter to pick up our mode of transportation. I'm always the planner for trips, so to just be along for the ride, literally, on this trip is incredible. We wheel our luggage out to the curb where our little car is waiting for us and hit the road in the bright Italian sunshine. As I settle into my seat and look around, I feel like I could either pass out or run a marathon as the adrenaline and sleepiness fight it out inside me. I make a mental promise to myself to stay awake to help Carter navigate our way to the villa. It's the least I can do after all the work he put into organizing this trip.

*

Good thing we're not actually in a cockpit together, because it turns out I am the world's worst navigator. The last thing I remember is pulling onto the highway after leaving the airport and now Carter is gently waking me up inside a garage.

"Oh shit, I'm so sorry," I say, coming to with a start. "I was going to help you find your way."

"It's okay," he says sweetly. "I had the route figured out before we left. I just used my headphones with my GPS directions so it wouldn't wake you. Kinda figured that drive would knock you out."

I smile and lean forward to kiss Carter before turning to get out of the car and help with bags. My internal clock is thoroughly confused though, and I am shocked to see it's still bright and sunny outside the garage.

"Bags can wait," he says. "I want to show you around."

I let Carter take me by the hand and step blinking into the sunlight before letting out the biggest gasp I have ever uttered. This place is everything I have ever dreamed of, and I can only see a tiny part of it. The villa is covered in vines but built with stone and brick that looks just the right amount of weathered. There are flowers all around the entryway and stairs lead up to an outdoor dining room table under a shaded awning.

Looking away from the house, I can see that we are up on a hill overlooking more hills covered with what appear to be wineries and unspoiled countryside. The air is warm and delicious, sweet-smelling, but not too perfumed. I realize I'm crying before I can even acknowledge the feelings of joy and relief. How could anyone be anything but completely relaxed in this beautiful place? No wonder the best art and music were created in this region of the world. How could you not be inspired?

Carter is leading me up the stairs to the entrance of the villa. The insides match the outsides perfectly. Everything is nicely appointed, but it still feels quaint and home-like. It is welcoming and pristine, all at the same time. The cool stone floors feel amazing as I kick off my shoes and leave them at the door. There are stairs directly in front of the door and I tiptoe up them for some reason. Quietly behind me, Carter is doing the same.

"Why are we being so quiet?" he whispers to me.

"Don't know," I whisper back. "Just felt like the right thing to do. I want the house to like us."

"Houses don't have feelings,"

"Oh yes, they do. Especially one this beautiful. Think about all she's seen."

"So, it's a girl now, is it?"

"Oh yes," I reply, reverently. "Can't you tell? Look how pretty she's made herself for us. She's practically preening."

Carter's hand is on my ass as he gives me a little pinch.

"Hey," I say in mock surprise. "Watch those hands, mister."

"Oh, I plan to," he says, catching up with me at the top of the stairs.

He follows me into the bedroom to the left, now touching me even more and nudging me toward the beautiful wrought iron bed. I resist just long enough to open the shutters and catch a glimpse of that view I could see from the ground level, which is even better from this height, but then turn back and stare at Carter. Even with the view behind me, this is what I want to look at right now. This incredible man who has brought me to this place I have always dreamed of seeing.

I quickly close the distance between us and kiss him hard, using my hands behind his head and neck to keep him pressed to me with an urgency I've never felt before. This is the kiss I've missed and subconsciously compared every other one to this year. It is equal parts familiar and exciting. We are electric.

I reluctantly pull apart from him long enough to pull my T-shirt over my head and let him do the same. We both also quickly take our pants off and kiss again in our underwear, still standing and pressing ourselves together as if we have magnets in our hips and shoulders. I feel his erection against me and reach down to stroke him gently with my hand. He moans in appreciation and I smile as his kisses move from my lips to my neck.

"Our first Italian sex," I say with a laugh. "I have a feeling it won't be our last."

"I didn't just bring you here to fuck," he says, unhooking my bra. As he slides the straps off and begins fondling my breasts, he smiles and adds, "but it's certainly on the agenda."

I laugh and fall backward onto the bed, pulling him down on top of me. As he kicks off his boxers, I slide off my underwear and open myself for him, physically and mentally. I can't help but flash back to everything that's gone on this year. Working out how I feel about this man might be the most crucial thing I decide for the rest of my life.

Before I can think too deeply on that matter, he is inside me and I want to cry. Or maybe I am crying. I definitely feel a tear on my cheek. I look up at Carter and realize it might actually be him, as he looks about as emotional as I feel. We lock eyes as he eases himself back and forth and I decide to break the intensity in the room by wrapping my legs around him and pulling him flat against me.

"Oh, so that's what you're in the mood for?" he says with a devilish laugh.

We're soon sweaty and exhausted as he finishes, still pressed against me. I'm thankful the window is open as a gentle breeze hits my skin. Maybe it's all the traveling, the relief I feel to be away from the madness at home, or just sheer post-coital bliss, but the last thing I remember is Carter kissing my forehead as I drift off for my second Italian nap.

*

The good news is I wake up feeling rested and energized. The bad news is I wake up at 10 p.m. local time and have officially done a terrible job of acclimating to my new surroundings. It is dark in the room and I'm alone, but a quick stumble to the window and I at least remember where the heck I am.

I let my eyes adjust to the lack of light and decide to search for Carter. There's a light on in the room downstairs and I smile as I take a few more steps and see his silhouette come into view. He's reading a novel and sitting on the couch, looking about as cozy and relaxed as I've ever seen him. Italy looks good on him, I decide.

"I think that's the first time I've ever seen you read something other than a textbook," I say quietly, hoping not to startle him.

"Ha, yeah, it probably is," he says. "I used to love to read, but I'm just always so tired from studying that I haven't done it nearly as much as I'd like to since we met. I'm kinda sad you don't know that about me." I must have made a face, because he quickly adds, "Not that it's your fault. I just haven't had a chance to show you that side of me before. But hey—isn't that what we're here for?"

I cross over to the couch and sit sideways on it so I'm facing him.

"Yes, that seems like a good use of our time," I say. "Speaking of which, how long are we here for?"

"The whole month," he says, smiling shyly. "I cleared it with Sam and she said she can absolutely hold down the fort, but she'll check in if she needs anything."

"Wow." I exhale a huge breath. "I can't believe you did this."

"Can't believe it in a good way?"

"In the best way," I say.

"Good," he says before letting out a huge yawn.

"Oh, no. Was I napping all alone up there? Our schedules are going to be totally out of whack."

"I tried to sleep for a bit, but realized the garage was still open and I wanted to get our things out of the car. And then I looked in the kitchen and thought I'd shop a bit while you rested so we'd have some food around, but I had fun exploring and stayed out longer than I'd planned. I left you a note, but you were out cold."

"Shoot. I can't believe I slept through our first day in Italy. Where are we, anyway?"

"Hang on." He gets up from the couch. "I can show you better on the map."

He walks across the room and picks up a three-ring binder that's on the bookshelf. It has an insert on the front with a picture of our little villa that says, "Welcome to Casa dei Fiordalisi." Inside the binder is a welcome letter from the owner, along with pages full of notes on Italian customs, recommendations for things to eat, see, and do, and in the front pocket, a map that Carter pulls out to show me where we are in relation to the rest of the region.

"We are in Trequanda which is right *here*," he says, pointing to the spot so easily that I can tell he's looked this up many times before. "We're about twenty miles from Siena and forty miles from Florence."

I look closer at the map and decide that if Italy were a thigh-high boot, we're just above the kneecap. From back in Arizona, I always pictured Italy somehow smaller than it now seems. And whereas a month seemed like a good amount of time to explore just a minute ago, I now feel like it's woefully inadequate. I want to see it all.

"I know what you're thinking," he says, interrupting my thoughts. "And the goal isn't to see it all. We're going to explore, but we're also going to relax. Besides, we have to leave some things to do for the next time we come."

I smile and sink back into the couch where Carter is opening his arms for me. He's tired and I'm practically tingling with energy. I want to kick myself.

"I packed some sleeping pills in case you want to try and get on Italy Time by tomorrow," he offers.

"Worth a shot," I say, standing to follow him as he leads us back up the stairs. I can't imagine they'll work with the amount of adrenaline coursing through my veins, but maybe I can read for a bit and get enough sleep to start tomorrow somewhat rested.

As we hit the second floor, I realize I am empty-handed and turn back to grab my bags.

"If you're looking for your suitcase, it's in here," Carter calls from the bedroom.

"My, what service!" I exclaim in a mocking tone as I enter the room. "Will you also be leaving mints on the pillow?"

"No mints, but how about some drugs? Or I can just hand them to you."

"Even better." I take the two pills he's offering me and throw them back with the water bottle from the nightstand.

We brush our teeth and get ready for bed together and it hits me how natural this feels. I usually don't feel comfortable in new settings for a day or two, and here I am, as far away from home as I've ever been, and everything is just fine. The ease between us would definitely go on my pro list, but I decided not to risk packing that lest we have a whole Ross/Rachel/Julie situation on our hands.

I grab the book I packed for the plane and climb into bed as Carter does the same on his side, albeit bookless.

"Goodnight," he says, giving me a sleepy kiss before falling heavily into his pillow.

"G'night," I say. "Thank you for bringing me here."

Before I can ask if he heard that, I am greeted with a gentle snore. Even on a regular night, he can always fall asleep faster than I can, but under the circumstances, I'm surprised he held on this long. I look down at my book, but the words on the page seem a bit fuzzy. Rubbing my eyes doesn't help, and after making a mental note to ask what brand of sleeping pills Carter gave me, I turn off the light, slide down under the covers and, for the third time today, fall into a deep Italian sleep.

Chapter Twenty-Three

June 2

Is there anything better than waking up without an alarm while gorgeous Tuscan sunshine streams in through the window? I honestly don't think so. And what is that smell wafting around the room? Italy is magical.

I roll over to find that Carter has already gotten up, so I turn the other way and gently put my feet on the cool stone floor. Outside the blanket, I actually feel a bit chilly, something I rarely get to experience in June as an Arizonan. I fumble through my bag to find a sweater and throw it on over my pajamas and go searching for my man and, to be honest, breakfast.

Coming down the stairs, I realize the delicious smell is getting stronger and start to wonder if Carter has taken our time apart to learn some new skills, but the kitchen appears empty and untouched.

Perplexed, I make my way out to the patio where I find him sitting with a few pastries and a cup of coffee, staring out at the rolling hills.

"Well, hello, Cyn-shine," he says, using his favorite nickname for me.

"*Buongiorno*," I say back. "Where did this lovely spread come from?"

"That would be the bakery next door," he says with a smile. "Can you smell it? I think we've hit the jackpot for location."

He is giddy and I can't help but match his mood. I've been so focused on how happy I am and what this trip means to me that I've forgotten what it must be like for him. He's worked so hard for so long, and after everything I've put him through this year, this must be incredibly overwhelming.

"Hey," I say, sitting in the chair next to him. "Have I told you yet how much I love this trip, and you for planning it? You're my hero."

We lock eyes for a few seconds while I try to convey how genuinely thankful I am, but then my stomach gives the loudest grumble I've ever heard and we both start to laugh. Carter gestures toward the plate of pastries and my stomach continues its roar.

"You should pick first," I say, then immediately hope he doesn't grab the one I'm eyeing.

"I've already had two," he says. "I may be a hero, but I'm no saint. And I wasn't sure how long you'd be sleeping. I couldn't resist the smells from next door."

"Aw, man." I grab the pastry covered in powdered sugar before he can go for number three. "How long have you been up? Did I sleep the day away?"

"I've only been up about fifteen minutes," he admits, dodging my fist as I reach over to lightly punch his arm. "But I really didn't know how long you'd sleep."

We break into laughter again and I am delighted that the pastry tastes as good as it looks. It's perfect for my first official Italian food. Light and fluffy, but so flavorful. I've been looking forward to the places and things we're going to see so much that I almost forgot about all the wonderful food we're going to eat.

"What's on the agenda today?" I ask, helping myself to another pastry.

"No agenda," he says. "I wasn't sure how we'd be feeling after traveling and getting settled, so I thought we could explore the town and make a game plan for the rest of the week, but we can do anything you like."

"That's very thoughtful of you," I say with a mouthful of another delicious treat. "I may go into a food coma after this breakfast, so a lazy day sounds delightful."

We sit and enjoy the scenery as we both happily savor the last of the baked goods. It is sunny and breezy, my two favorite elements for exploring, and my legs are itching to get moving.

"Do we have bikes?" I ask, struck with inspiration.

"There are some in the garage we can use," Carter says. "Looking to cover more ground than we can on foot?"

"I just feel like riding bikes through the Italian countryside is so very perfect and that's what we should do. Right now."

"Right now?" He grins.

"Well, maybe we should change first, but pretty much now, yeah."

We clear the plate and head inside to get ready. I run upstairs to brush my teeth, throw my hair up in a ponytail, add some sunscreen moisturizer to my face, put on shorts and a tank top, and head back down to find Carter getting the bikes pulled out and ready to go.

"Do we need the map?" I ask, thinking back on my Girl Scout days. "And maybe a compass?"

"I think we'll be okay if we don't go too far," says Carter, who honestly has terrible survival instincts. I grab my phone and take a picture of the map from the binder and double check that my compass app works without Wi-Fi. It does, and I feel a bit better, seeing as how we're about to set out in an area where we don't speak the language and have never been before.

I close the door behind me and bounce my way down the steps, excited to see more of our beautiful surroundings. Carter has thrown a couple of water bottles in the basket of his bike and has a huge smile on his face, likely mirroring mine.

I throw my leg over my bike and teeter a little before finding my balance. The bike is old but sturdy and I soon feel like a kid again as I pick up speed and the breeze blows harder in my face. Carter is behind me, but just a bit, so I slow down until we're side by side.

"Which way?" I ask as we pull up to a fork in the road. I look up at the street sign and try to remember the name of it, but we're right on the edge of the town and I feel like I'll remember how this looks.

"Well, left takes us more into town, but I think right takes us toward the next village."

"Hmmm. Town?" I suggest.

"Town it is," he says, leading the way. I take out my phone for a minute and find that we are heading northeast, meaning our villa must be on the southwest corner of town. I make a mental note and pedal after Carter.

We wind our way through the streets and soon find ourselves in the town square, where the local church is truly something to behold. If the church in this tiny town is this pretty, I can't wait to see the others in the bigger cities we'll visit. The bricks are alternating colors, giving it a mesmerizing checkerboard feel. I'm lost in thought and just sitting on my bike seat until a voice pulls me back to reality.

"I'm sorry?" I say, realizing there's a gentleman standing on my right.

"Ahh, American," he says. "I say you like our church, yes?"

"Oh yes. It's lovely. The whole town is."

He appears a little confused but smiles and nods before going on his way. I look across the square to see Carter investigating the church more closely and smile. He turns to see me as I gesture to keep going and we make our way down another street. It's mostly houses, but there's a little market, another bakery, a pharmacy, and two restaurants I'm sure we'll check out later. It's still early, so they aren't open, but we stop in the market for a loaf of bread and some meat and cheese to add to our basket.

"Oh shoot," I say, as we hop back on the bikes. "I should have brought a blanket or something to lay down so we can have a little picnic."

"Eh, we'll make do," he says.

On we go until we reach the edge of town, so we decide to head toward the fields stretching to the south. I'm thankful I have the compass as I check again to make sure I have my bearings. The road is rockier and dustier than it was in town, so we slow our pace a bit, but as we wind in and out of shady areas and brilliant sunshine, I don't mind at all. I'm not sure how long we've been riding when Carter comes to a stop a few feet ahead of me.

"Everything okay?" I ask, stopping next to him.

"Better than okay," he says. "Look."

I follow along his hand to where he's pointing and spot a little stream winding its way through the trees. It could not be more picturesque, so I understand why he wanted me to see it. Then I squint and realize why he looks so excited. A small bench sits just above the stream and it's like God heard we didn't have a blanket, so he made us our own little picnic spot.

"Ahh," I sigh. "Better than okay for sure."

We walk the bikes down the grassy area and rest them on a tree near the bench before unloading our food. Our meats and cheese are wrapped in paper, which we carefully unfold to have somewhere to put the bread before digging in. I have no idea what everything is, but it's all so delicious that I don't care. I don't even feel like talking as I savor each bite and watch the stream dance its way over rocks and dips in the land. A few bugs come around to investigate, but none are too bothersome, so I don't even go into my usual swatting frenzy.

"Is everything here like a storybook?" Carter wonders aloud.

"All evidence points to yes so far," I say, finishing the last of the cheese on my side of the bench. "It's so quaint and lovely. Are you sure we only get to stay a month?"

"I was thinking the same thing. I mean, how much do I really want to be a doctor in America anyway? I should see if I can transfer to some Italian school."

"Yes, that makes sense." I nod. "And I'm pretty sure my ice cream skills will transfer to gelato-making. Oh my God. We have to get gelato."

Carter laughs at my abrupt mood shift, but I don't care. I suddenly cannot wait to try every flavor of gelato I can and now have no bigger goal on our trip. I should really make a note of everything we try.

"I've lost you, haven't I?" he says.

"Who, me? No, no," I say. "I was just thinking I should get a note-book to jot down all of the flavors we try, but I'm back. Really."

"It's okay. I love when you go all ice cream nerd on me."

The food is gone, so I crumple up the paper in my hand and close the gap between us.

"Good thing, cuz I'm going to seriously geek out," I say, kissing him. "It might be like Vermont all over again."

"If I recall, good things happened in Vermont," he says, kissing me back. "I'd be okay with a repeat."

Long story short, I got *really* excited on our tour of the Ben and Jerry's facility and Carter was the beneficiary of all that extra energy. He still refers to it as our foursome because of how influential two other men were to our sex that night.

All this thought of gelato and a steamy night in New England long ago has me seriously turned on, and since we're a bit off the path and relatively secluded, I wrap my legs around Carter and kiss him even harder. I begin to wonder if this bench has ever seen this kind of action before, but I get the feeling it has inspired at least some heavy make-out sessions by the local teenagers.

Carter's hands dig into my hips as we come even closer together and I feel him look back toward the road to see if anyone is around before he pulls down my tank top to kiss my breasts. I moan, encour-aging him as he pulls my top down even lower to bring my left breast into his mouth. I'm sweaty and a bit sticky, but everything feels too good for me to stop. I shift around on his lap to grind into him a little more.

That's all the encouragement he needs to stand up and bring us both to the other side of the bench, so we're now behind a tree and out of sight from the road. We kiss furiously as we reach down to unbutton our shorts and soon we are both half-dressed and fucking up against a tree. Kindly, the tree has very soft bark, so I'm not even scratching up my back as Carter thrusts harder and harder. Okay, maybe I'm scratching my back a little.

"Hang on," I say, pulling myself off him and turning around. I bend over so that my hands are on the bench, but we're still pretty hidden from view. My top is still pulled down, so I'm still a bit exposed, but it's hot as hell and I let out a small gasp as Carter enters me again. His sweat drips on my back as he leans forward to fondle my tits with one hand while reaching down to my clit with the other.

"Come with me," he says and I happily oblige, exploding with a super intense orgasm as he finishes into the bush behind the bench.

"Figured our ride home would be pretty uncomfortable if you were all sticky," he says after shuddering his last after-sex shudder.

"Such a gentleman," I say, using the outside of the food paper to clean myself up a bit before getting dressed again. "For someone who didn't just bring me to Italy for sex, I'd say you're getting a lot of it."

"It wasn't the main thing, but it's certainly not the worst way to pass the time."

I laugh and slap him lightly on the butt as he pulls his shorts up.

"Thanks for the sex," I say. "Good game."

Any butt-slapping between us is always an inside joke about dudes who play sports. I always feel like that's such a weird thing for jocks to do to each other, so the first time I did it to Carter, we both cracked up and it's been going ever since. He pats me back and adds, "You too."

We each take some big gulps of our water, put the bottles and our trash in the basket, and get ready to hit the road again for more exploring. I look around before we leave to see if there is any way to easily find this spot again, but I have no idea how Carter found it in the first place, so I just snap a selfie of us there before we take off.

We come across another little town a way down the road, but it's even smaller than Trequanda, so there's not too much to see. A nice woman sitting in front of her house notices that our water bottles are low and through a mini game of charades, we realize she is offering to fill them for us. We thank her in our limited Italian and I'm pretty sure I butcher the pronunciation of *grazie mille,* but she smiles and seems delighted that we tried.

As we leave the town, we come to a fork in the road and Carter starts heading to the right.

"Oh, did you want to keep going? I thought we might head back to the villa," I say.

"This *is* the way to the villa," he says, oddly confident.

"Actually, it's this way. We have to head back north."

"North? How do you know which way is north?"

"I've been using my compass." I hope this doesn't undermine his masculinity or something.

"Brilliant. I was worried I'd get us lost. You lead the way."

I smile and wonder how I even thought I needed to hide the fact that I didn't want us to get lost. Maybe it's our time apart, but I have always known Carter appreciates my intelligence. He's much smarter than I am, but in more of a book smarts way. We're a good team.

I lead us back down the road that takes us to Trequanda, keeping an eye out for the little bench by the stream. I miss it though, and it's not long before we're pulling back into the town square. I pause again to look at the church, which is even prettier in the later afternoon sunshine, when a smell hits my nose. I know immediately that I must investigate it. I turn around to see Carter a few feet behind me and clearly noticing the delicious smell also.

We get off the bikes to walk them through the square as we pull a Toucan Sam and follow our noses. Quickly, we walk down a little side street until we are at one of the two restaurants in town, Pizza Paradiso. We park our bikes on the wall outside and stroll in through the patio where I hold up two fingers to indicate how many people will be in our party.

The hostess says something in Italian that sounds very welcoming, guides us to our table, and hands us our menu. Everything is in Italian, but I feel like we can figure it out. Besides, I want whatever it is I can smell, so I trust them to send us out something delicious.

When our waiter appears, we quickly apologize and say we don't speak Italian. I'm completely ready to bust out my charade skills again, but he speaks English and asks what we'd like to drink.

"Can you bring us whatever wine and pizza you like best?" Carter says, then looking quickly at me, "if that's okay with you?"

"Sounds great," I say.

As he takes our menus, I realize there was a back side filled with desserts that we didn't check out. I turn my head to look back inside the restaurant and see a sign reading "Gelateria."

Carter follows my gaze, then turns to me and smiles. "Should we ask our waiter for paper and a pen so you can start your notes?"

"Nah, I think I can remember one flavor until we get back to the house," I say.

I sit back in my chair a bit and sigh, feeling a mix of peace, hunger, anticipation, and gratitude. I cannot believe how different it feels to be here, when just forty-eight hours ago I was home and completely jumbled. I will never be able to thank Carter enough for this trip.

And what if we don't end up together? Will this trip be the end of our years-long relationship and the best goodbye ever? The thought makes me want to cry. Haven't I always dreamed of finding a man who understands me so well he could plan a dream trip for me? And isn't that man sitting right across from me?

As the waiter brings us a bottle of red wine and two glasses, I make a decision. For the duration of this trip, I am going to treat Carter like he is the one for me and no one else exists. If that feels completely right by the time we head back home, I can see no reason to pick back up with The Plan. And this time, I won't let him talk me back into finishing it out.

I raise my glass to the man sitting across from me, look him directly in the eye, and say, "To us."

"To us," he says, looking at me with the same intensity. Did he just have the same thought I did?

Our pizza arrives before I can ask him, and all complicated relationship thoughts go out of my mind as I take in the beautiful food on our table.

"Prosciutto crudo," our waiter says, naming the pizza as he sets it down between us. I repeat the phrase in my head a few times, hoping to lock it into my memory for future reference. Then I take a bite and realize that won't be a problem. I will never, ever forget the name of this. And I will never, ever be able to eat crappy pizza back home again.

We take our time finishing the entire thing and the whole bottle of wine until I'm deliriously full and tipsy. Our waiter brings back the menus, dessert side up, and I close my eyes and point to something, once again trusting that anything from this establishment will be wonderful. I open my eyes to see that my finger landed on sorbetto prosecco and smile. I don't know if that means it's sorbet flavored like prosecco or maybe sorbet with prosecco poured around it, but I don't care. Either sounds amazing. I should tell Carter how amazing everything is.

"Everything is amazing," I say. "You, this food, this place. Amazing. And remember when we had sex by the stream. Ah-mazing."

"I think someone's a little drunk," he replies, slurring a little. "Or maybe two someones."

"Not drunk." I shake my head. "Jus' a little tipsy."

"I love tipsy Cynthia." He hiccoughs.

"And she loves tipsy Carter." I smile serenely. Or, at least, it feels serene. I'm probably making drunk-idiot face.

The waiter brings back our dessert and I giggle as I see that mine is a red sorbet (raspberry, by the look of it) with prosecco poured around it. I taste it (yup—raspberry!) and let out an "mm" that feels like it will never end.

Carter got a traditional gelato with a little wafer sticking out of it. "Mm," he says, taking his first bite. "I think this is salted caramel."

"What was it called?" I ask, taking another delicious bite of mine.

"No idea. Told you we should have gotten paper."

We both push our desserts across the table for the other to take a bite and give another "mm," this time in unison. I'd laugh, but it's more reverent than funny. This is like the church of food. And I'm the newest convert.

I finish my sorbet, then drink the rest of the prosecco in the glass, giggling a little as the bubbles go down my throat. This was one of the best days of my life and I can't stop smiling.

"Thank you for bringing me here," I say, reaching out to grab Carter's hand.

"Thank you for coming with me," he says. "I had so much fun planning this trip, but part of me was worried you wouldn't come. I've been planning since January and had to keep telling myself I might be coming here alone, but I kept going with you in mind. So, thank you. I'd be a bit lonely here by myself. And that whole thing by the stream would have been downright creepy without you."

I laugh so hard prosecco comes out my nose. It kinda burns, but it makes me laugh harder. I'm laughing so hard that people from other tables are looking, but I don't care. We've paid our bill, so I nod toward the exit, and we make our way back to the bikes, laughing the whole way out. I hope we haven't embarrassed ourselves too much, as I definitely want to go back there.

Looking at the bikes and assessing my state of inebriation, I make the judgment call to start walking alongside my bike. Carter does the same and we wind our way back to the edge of town, nodding and saying hello to everyone we pass. I notice there are a lot of people out and about, unlike this morning when we barely saw anyone. I look at Carter, about to comment on it, when he beats me to it.

"*Passeggiata*," he says. "It's an evening stroll that is really common in Italy."

"Oh," I say. "I love it. Let's get the bikes back to the house and join them, shall we?"

We do and I am immediately in love with this idea. Why don't we do this at home? It seems like the whole town is out and about, greeting each other and catching up in the town square and down each street. We hold hands and listen in on conversations we can't understand, but there's a beauty in this kind of community gathering that transcends language.

I am no longer tipsy after we've walked through the whole town and am surprised at how not full and lazy I feel. Normally when I eat so many carbs in a day, I just want to curl up and sleep. Is the bread here magical too?

We make our way back to Casa dei Fiordalisi and enter through the main door connecting our villa to the rest of the town. I didn't realize the garage is actually at the back of the house and wonder now what so many of the homes in this village look like from the other side. We'll have to take a different route on our next passeggiata.

As we walk in, I nearly gasp as I see how the sunset has changed the colors inside and on the patio. We walk through and take in the view in total silence. The hills, so green and brown when I've looked at them before, almost seem like they are on fire now. The sky is the most vibrant shades of pink, orange, and purple I've ever seen.

"It looks like a symphony," I exhale. "No wonder composers wrote such beautiful music here."

"And painters," says Carter. "They were just trying to capture it all as best they could."

"Yeah," is all I can say.

The sun finally sets completely, and we make our way up to the bedroom, exhausted after a long, wonderful day. There will be nights, I know, when we keep exploring, but for now, there is only sleep.

Chapter Twenty-Four

June 7

We branch out over the next few days to the surrounding cities and towns, finding each as lovely as the last. And I wasn't kidding about the food. It's all amazing.

First on our list is Siena, one of the larger cities in the area. I can tell as we drive in that it is huge compared to our little Trequanda, but walking through the streets makes it seem just as quaint. Or so I think until we turn a corner and find the large church in the middle of the city. The Siena Duomo, or Siena Cathedral, is breathtaking. I mean, I literally gasped when we saw it. I couldn't stop staring at it.

It has a really cool striped pattern along the sides and this gorgeous door on the front. We didn't take the official tour, so I can't tell you the history or any of the materials, but it's just so cool looking. There's also this really big sun over the door that surprised me. I wish I'd asked what it meant.

"Uh, did you want to go inside?" Carter asks, pulling me from my thoughts.

"Sure," I say, though I know I could have stared at the outside for hours.

The inside is even more magnificent, and we both take our time examining all the paintings and intricate carvings throughout. I still don't know what a lot of it means or who made it, but I know how it makes me feel, and that's what counts. Well, to me anyway.

"Am I allowed to light a candle?" I whisper to Carter, gesturing toward the pretty little tea lights grouped in sections around the church.

"Uh, I think so?" comes his quiet reply. "It looks like they have a spot for donations. I don't see why not."

I approach the nearest group of candles, drop a euro in the box, and pick up a candle. But then, I blank on what to pray for. Safe travels for our trip? Guidance on my quest to find true love this year? Does God really want to help someone who is currently being protested by religious people? And that's when it hits me.

Under my breath, I mutter the following as I use the flame of another candle to light my own.

"Hi, God. It's me. Could you please heal the hearts of the people who hate me back home? Give them whatever peace they need so that they don't have to put me down to feel better about themselves. Maybe tell them I'm actually pretty nice? And please keep Meg and the baby safe. And if you have time, I'd love a sign or two about what I'm supposed to be doing. Thanks, and amen."

Satisfied that I haven't offended the nice nuns or whoever set the candles out, I place my candle down with the rest of them and smile. That felt nice.

We hit the streets of Siena again, blinking in the bright sunlight. There are restaurants near the Duomo, but one thing I've learned while traveling is to get a bit of distance from the touristy areas of a place if you want to find the good food. Or at least not get ripped off.

We make our way back toward the center of town when I again smell something really delicious.

"Is that Chinese food?" says Carter.

"Sure smells like it," I say, turning in a circle to try to find the source.

We both see it at the same time: a Chinese flag hanging above the doorway of a little restaurant. The menu in the front window has pictures and now that we have a visual to match the smell, we decide to go in.

I never thought I'd have the best Chinese food of my life in Siena, Italy, but darn if we don't have some seriously delicious food there. Soup, dumplings, multiple meat and rice dishes. All served by the sweetest Chinese couple, who we also hear serving a couple in the corner in Italian after taking our order in English. I wish I had thought to ask them their story, but I somehow know they've lived an interesting life.

Exploring the rest of the city is much easier on a full stomach, especially when we get to the town square and decide to climb the bell tower of the Palazzo Pubblico, which gives us a beautiful view of Piazza del Campo and all of Siena. Climbing tall structures will soon become a main staple in each town we visit, making my emphasis on eating all the good food that much more important.

Similarly, I easily talk Carter into rewarding our hard work up and down the tower with gelato, which I keep track of in the notebook I picked up at a local gift shop. My *stracciatella* was quite good, while Carter's banana was also yummy.

The next day, we take a similar tour around Montepulciano, where I nerdily point out the church where they filmed part of the *Twilight* movies. Carter threatens to ditch me if I ever mention that again, so I take a selfie behind his back before we look for a place for lunch.

On our way to find food, we stumble across a wine cellar offering tours and tastings. We take about a second to think about it before walking in and pretending to care how it all works before the good part: tasting. Well, Carter probably cares more than I do about how it works, but I am pretty much focused on the actual drinking part. I am not disappointed, and we end up purchasing six bottles, which the owner kindly offers to hold on to for us while we continue our exploration of his town.

Another fabulous lunch (hello, gnocchi!), and a quick (actually, not so quick) climb of their bell tower and we feel like we have covered enough ground to call it a day. As it's still early, we grab our wine, head back to the villa, and take ourselves a nap. After passing out early each day, exhausted from all the exploring and long evening strolls, I told Carter the only way we'd ever experience Italian nightlife would be for me to nap.

It's brilliant. With no set time that we have to be anywhere, we fall asleep together on top of the covers, warm enough to feel perfectly comfortable. When the afternoon breeze changes through the window, I wake with goose bumps, and realize they are also coming from Carter, awake and gently caressing my arm.

Lazily, I roll toward him and kiss him. His hand moves from my arm to my legs, where he quickly goes from caressing my thigh to moving upward under the skirt of my dress. I smile as he wastes no time in moving my panties to the side and begins exploring my wetness.

"Well, someone woke up in a good mood," I say, moaning a bit as he puts one finger fully inside me, still stroking around with his thumb on my clit.

"I woke up and saw you there and thought I'd be a gentleman and let you sleep," he says, moving his hand on and inside me faster now. "But then I thought, 'nah, she's slept long enough.'"

"Indeed, I have," I say, lying back and letting him continue. I'm wearing a light, button-down summer dress and lace bralette, so I use my free hands to unbutton and pull my dress open a bit. Carter needs no invitation and props himself up on his free arm. He leans down to kiss me on the mouth first before inching his way down my neck and onto my chest. He gently licks and plays with my nipples over the lace and the feeling sets me on fire. The combination of that and his expert handiwork on my clit soon bring me to climax.

"Mmmm, fuck me," I say as my body stops shivering.

He pulls his shorts and boxers down with Superman-like speed, then lifts my skirt a little higher. Carter climbs on top of me and thrusts into me with urgency. I wonder how long he'd been hard and waiting for me, but don't ask in case it broke his concentration.

"Hang on," I say, realizing I have quite the visual opportunity here. "Roll over."

Dropping to his back faster than a speeding bullet, Carter looks at me with anticipation as I climb on top of him and begin riding him with intensity. I reach up to grab the headboard for greater control and bring myself up and down in circular motions, enjoying the hell out of the face he's making.

"Oh, fuck yes," he says. "You look so fucking hot."

This is exactly what I was going for. Half dressed, with my breasts covered in lace, on top and totally into it: I knew Carter would love it. I catch a glimpse of us in the mirror and am even more turned on when I see the picture we made.

We have made love many times before, had sex on countless

occasions, but every once in a while, there's only one word for it: fucking. We are going hard, and it feels great. Carter reaching his hands up to caress my breasts only increases my intense pleasure.

"Harder," I moan, shrieking slightly when he pinches my nipples. A few more thrusts and I see Carter's O face just before I feel him explode inside me. I lean down, not bothering to hop off just yet, and kiss him passionately.

"Damn," he says. "We should really nap more often."

Chapter Twenty-Five

June 11

Soon, the days begin to melt into each other as we fall into a rhythm and daily routine. With no set times that we have to be anywhere, we could easily have slept in each day and let the time drift away, but we both wake as soon as the sunlight hits our faces in the morning, ready to face that day's adventures. We get into the habit of making general plans for our days the night before, so we at least have a sense of purpose as we stretch and yawn in the breezy bedroom. Sleeping with the window open wearing nothing each night in Italy is something I highly recommend, by the way.

We've mostly been sticking to areas close to Trequanda, so there is no need to rush, but on the days when we have to set alarms or stick to schedules, we find ourselves just as eager to rise and shine. One of those days is our day spent in Florence, where we want to arrive early for a full day of sightseeing, food, and art. We booked tickets in advance for the Uffizi, and as we pass the long entrance line that wraps around the building, I'm thankful we had.

"We'd better book our Rome tours in advance," Carter says to me as we watch a tourist in line struggle to get a Romani woman to leave her alone.

"You can say that again," I says, making a mental note of all the places in Rome I want to see.

I quickly forget about Rome as we walk the halls, taking in paintings, sculptures, and all kinds of beauty from the different eras of Italian art. Just when I think we must be toward the end of the museum, we turn another corner and I see that we've only scratched the surface. It's equal parts breathtaking and overwhelming. It's hard to appreciate any one painting when there are hundreds more to divert your attention.

After getting our culture on and feeling quite refined, we hop on a double-decker bus to see more of the city. Compared to the warm, crowded museum, this is much more my scene. I love architecture and Florence is an absolutely stunning city. We get a great view of the famous bridge at Point Vecchio and decide to hop off the tour to explore the area a bit more. We wind in and out of stalls where vendors sell their wares. I am trying on a pair of sunglasses in one of the shops when I catch Carter's gaze in my reflection.

"What are you thinking about, staring like that?" I ask, turning around.

"Just that even with all the beautiful things I've seen today, this is my favorite view," he says.

"Careful, mister," I tease. "Talk like that is going to make me blush."

But it's too late. I know my cheeks are pink under his gaze and don't really care. I have started to call that look his "Italy eyes." Maybe it's just how everyone looks at someone they love in such a beautiful place. Maybe it's our time apart that makes him see me in a new way. Either way, I have never felt more beautiful than I do seeing myself through his eyes.

We hop back on the bus and make our way to the center of town where we have lunch in the shadow of the Duomo. Speaking of beautiful views, I find myself openly gaping at it as I sip wine and lean back in my chair.

"You're so much happier outside here than in, aren't you?" Carter says, laughing as I dribble a bit of wine down my chin in my stupor.

"How could anyone want to be inside on a day like today?" I reply. "I mean, the museum was great, but just look at this place."

"So, you don't want to go inside? And we should just skip David?"

"No, no. You know I love the inside of these cathedrals. And I've got to meet David."

The David sculpture also resides in Florence and I really am looking forward to seeing it. We've been joking for days that you can't really say you've been to Italy if you don't meet David. There are other things on our list that we still need to do, but we've talked about the David as if he were a real person and I can only hope that "meeting" him will live up to my expectations. We'd discovered on our arrival that there are replicas of him throughout the city, but that doesn't mean I want to skip the real thing.

And so, we made our way to the Academia Gallery after walking through the Cathedral de Santa Maria del Fiore, which we discover is the Duomo's full name. It is striking and lovely as all Italian churches have been thus far, but I know we have a new friend to meet.

Walking through the Academia Gallery makes me feel genuinely sad for every piece of art housed there that is not named David. Michelangelo's masterpiece is even more magnificent than I could have imagined, and it makes every other sculpture there seem less amazing by comparison. You first view David from about a hundred feet away and it's clear just how massive a sculpture it is, even from that distance. But as you walk slowly toward it, you start to realize just how incredible it is in both size and skill.

"Wow," breathes Carter as we make our way toward him through the molasses-like crowd.

"Hi, David," I say. "We've been looking forward to meeting you."

A tourist nearby who must also speak English turns to give me a weird glance, but I don't care. This is so cool to see, and I don't care who hears my reverent greeting.

"His eyes are facing Rome," says Carter. "Look how defiant he looks."

I smile, happy that Carter has done his research.

"He's like us," I say. "Clearly, no one can hurt him here, but he's daring anyone who would try."

My mind wanders for a moment back to home and the life we're escaping from on this trip. I make a mental note to check in with Sam soon and post an update on the blog before bringing my attention back to the here and now.

"Take care, David," I say as we make our way into the next section of the museum.

"Sorry for staring at your junk," says Carter, causing us both to break into giggling fits. We get a few glares from the staff, but we both make like David and defiantly stare back.

Chapter Twenty-Six

June 13

After taking a day to relax and lounge around the villa after our long day in Florence, we again set our alarms, but this time even earlier. I may have protested briefly about getting up at 4:00 a.m., but when Carter showed me pictures of where we were headed, I decided I could lose a bit of sleep. After getting dressed, throwing on my tennis shoes, and grabbing the bags we packed the night before, I sleepily follow Carter to the car, whining only for a second that the sun isn't even up yet.

"Trust me, it'll be coming up when we get there," he assures me.

Seeing as it isn't up yet, I take the long trip ahead of us as a chance to sleep a bit more, only waking up as the drive takes us down winding, narrow roads. We are clearly driving through hills and as we come up and over them, I see the Italian Riviera for the first time and gasp.

Carter was right: the sun is coming up on our arrival and as I look out on the water and see the early morning sun dancing upon it, I want to cry.

"Cinque Terre," Carter says, clearly as awed as I was.

"Which town are we starting in?" I asked.

"Monterosso al Mare," he replied. "We'll park there and hike through the rest."

As we find a place to leave the car, I look back up at the cliffs and try to see the next town we'll find on our journey, but it's hidden from view at this angle. We're near the beach of Monterosso and I see beautiful chairs along the sand, which appear to also have service from a restaurant. Suddenly, the thought of hiking through these cliffs seems like the dumbest idea ever.

"Trust me," says Carter, clearly reading my mind, "you'll be glad you did this."

I throw my backpack on my shoulders, take a few pictures, play hopscotch on the sidewalk where the numbers have been etched in the concrete, then decide I've dawdled enough and follow him to the head of the trail.

As we head up a bit, I keep looking back to see where we've been. Each step up gives me a new vantage point and I can't help but wonder how anything else we'll see today could possibly compare. The blue on the water is an impossible shade of teal. That sand we just left looks stark white, soft, and so inviting. Why didn't I think to go into the water? The cliffs continue and seem to be the most perfect shade of green I've ever seen, with the little town of Monterosso fitting so perfectly in the façade that it looks like it has been there always.

We somehow seem to be only going up and my legs are already sore. Not a great sign for the first piece of a four-part hike. But as we make our way up the mountain, I start to see how beautiful the hike actually is. Steps are carved into the rocks here and there, vines with grapes that seem to be as unkempt and wild as I feel in this moment, and enough shade to make a quick rest every now and again feel luxurious. The trail isn't wide, but it's surrounded by other land, so I don't even mind how high up we are. That is, until we come to an impossibly narrow section on the side of the cliff.

My eyes dart around for another way to go, but I soon realize this is the path. It's about the width of both of my feet if I have them right next to each other and it's clearly the way we're supposed to go, but my heart races as I make the stupid mistake of looking down.

"You can do this," Carter says, sensing my anxiety.

"Well, if I'm going to die, I suppose this is as good a place as any," I say, masking my terror with humor.

Carter steps out on the ledge-trail before me and makes it look easy, quickly getting across the fifteen-foot section like it's a balance beam. I take a deep breath, then follow him quickly, nearly bursting into tears when I get to the other side.

"That. Had. Better. Be. The. Only. Section. Like. That," I say between breaths.

"It is," he says, taking me in his arms. "I actually can't believe you did it. I was worried we'd have to turn around and take the train."

"There's a *train*?" I exclaim. "And you knew about this section??"

"We'll take the train back," he says quickly. "But I know you'll be happy we hiked the whole way there. And yes, I knew, but the guide says it's the only scary part. The rest is just one foot in front of the other and I know you can do it."

I secretly make plans to murder Carter later, but decide I'd better let him live for the moment. He is, after all, carrying the water in his backpack. We make our way up and up, with me singing "Climb Ev'ry Mountain," from *The Sound of Music* between breaths to both pass the time and mask my plans to kill him, when the trail evens out and I realize we've gone as high as we possibly can. As the trail starts to go back down, Carter lets out a quiet gasp in front of me. Catching up to him on the trail, I soon know why.

While I was looking back at our last views of Monterosso, Carter was looking down at our first glimpse of the second town on our journey: Vernazza. It is so beautiful I can barely believe it's real. With brightly colored buildings that, like Monterosso, seem to be part of the very cliffs themselves, Vernazza is a stunning vision. The waves crash on the rocky alcove where boats seem to come and go, and I laugh to myself for believing the only way to get between each of these towns was to hike.

"What's so funny?" Carter asks.

"We could have taken a boat," I say, laughing harder. "Or a train."

"But neither of those things would give you this view," he says, turning and pulling me into his arms. "You earned this view and I'm so glad you're here with me to see it."

I let him kiss me, softly at first, before answering back with a more intense kiss of my own. He's right. I am proud of myself for taking the scenic route. It truly is the most beautiful day of my life. How many things have I missed because I've been too scared to try them? Or because I took the easy way?

We hike down to Vernazza, holding hands when the trail is wide enough, and I'm in awe of the different views we see on the way down. It becomes more beautiful the closer we get until we are in the streets of the town itself. We stop at a bakery for a few delicious breakfast treats and find a shady bench overlooking the water.

"Can I ask you something?" Carter says, hesitantly. I nod, my mouth full of food, so he continues. "Do you feel like you really even know those other guys?"

"Don't," I say, swallowing my last bite of pastry. "Don't bring them here with us. Not today."

"They're here with us whether I bring them up or not. I've just been wondering how much you could even really know about any of them after only a month."

"Well, I have been asking each of them a few questions to get to

know them better. I ask the same ones each time. It's my own little com-
patibility test, I guess."

"Do you want to ask me the questions?"

"I think I already know your answers,"

"Then let's see if you do," he says, standing and taking my hand.

So, all through the next part of our hike between Vernazza and
Corniglia, we dive into a *Newlywed Game* version of my interview questions.

1. Given the choice of anyone in the world, who would you want
as a dinner guest? (I guess that Carter would choose Yadier Molina or
one of the other St. Louis Cardinals that he loves. "Yeah, maybe," he
says, thinking it over. "It would probably be an athlete. I don't know
that I'd want to have a whole dinner with them or anything, but I'd
love to meet the whole team. Not sure what all we'd talk about though.
Dinner is a long time." I laugh, imagining my sweet, introverted Carter
trying to make conversation over several courses and realize I should
have known this would be a tough one. "Well, if that ever happens,
hopefully I'll be there to help you through it," I say. He smiles and
squeezes my hand.)

2. Would you like to be famous? In what way? ("Not at all," I answer for him. "I think you'd like to be well-known among your peers
for being a good person and a good doctor, but actual fame would be a
nightmare for you." He smiles, shudders, and says, "You've got that
right.")

3. Before making a telephone call, do you ever rehearse what you are going to say? Why? ("I'm torn on this one," I confess. "I feel like you do this for business and school related things, but not for calls to friends and family. Am I close?" Carter takes a minute to think about his answer, which makes me think I've got it wrong. "I remember doing this the first time I called you. The first few times, actually." "Really?" I say. "Well, yeah. I wanted to make sure I made a good impression. I wasn't sure if we were on the same page and I didn't want you to get the wrong idea, so I practiced sounding less into you than I was. Kind of a dick move, looking back." We both laugh, especially as I remember thinking he did, in fact, sound like a bit of a dick at first.)

4. What would constitute a "perfect" day for you? ("Today," we both say in unison. "Every day of this trip, really," he adds, "but today is especially perfect so far." We both look at our surroundings, and I ignore the pain in my legs and chest from all this hiking long enough to nod in agreement. "One of the most beautiful places in the world with one of my favorite people," he says, squeezing my hand again.)

5. When did you last sing to yourself? To someone else? ("You were probably drunk," I say, trying to think when the last time I heard him sing was. "Or maybe it was on my birthday?" Carter doesn't sing nearly as often as I do, although he really does have a lovely voice. "Nope," he says with a smile. "It was the other night after you'd fallen asleep. I sang a bit of 'Better Together' by Jack Johnson while I watched you." Well heck. That's pretty darn sweet.)

6. If you were able to live to the age of ninety and retain either the mind or body of a thirty-year-old for the last sixty years of your life, which would you want? ("You would say mind. I'm 100 percent sure," I say confidently. "Well, yeah," he says. "Although, working with people who can no longer get around like they used to makes me think body might be the better answer. But even if I couldn't get around as easily as I can today, I could still use that sharp mind of mine to help people, so yeah, I guess I'll go with mind. These are tough questions.")

7. Do you have a secret hunch about how you will die? ("About thirty minutes ago, it was going to be me pushing you off this mountain," I say with a laugh. "Uh, yeah, I noticed," he says. "How?" I ask. "You don't hide your emotions very well. Not from me, anyway. I saw that murder-face you were shooting at me. But otherwise? Hopefully old and warm in my bed, with you by my side." It's a sweet answer, but the sudden thought of losing him makes everything more real than I want it to be. "I demand to go first," I say defiantly. "Okay," he says. "But I'll be right behind you.")

8. Name three things you and your partner appear to have in common. ("I think you'd say we're both smart, funny and fit," I say. "Well, those are true," he says, "but I think I'd go a little deeper if I were trying to convince you that we're compatible." "Fair enough," I reply. "Because we're not just smart," he continues. "We both value being smart. I think that's an important distinction. Neither of us could ever be with someone who doesn't at least try to think things through. And we're

not just funny; we're funny to each other. We have a very similar sense of humor. It makes watching movies and TV shows that much better. And I wouldn't have gone with fit, although I do appreciate your body," he says, giving my butt a quick squeeze. "I'd say we're both generous. I love how giving you are with your time and your kindness. You make me want to be a better man.")

9. For what in your life do you feel most grateful? ("I think you'd say…" I try to think for a minute. What is Carter most thankful for? He's got a pretty good life, his health, a good career coming up once school is over. I don't want to be conceited and say it's me, but this trip has made me think it might just be me after all. I stop walking for a second to look at him, trying to read his mind. "I think you know what it is," he says, looking at me seriously. "It's my Xbox." We both laugh and even though I know he's kidding I don't press for a real answer. It may not be me yet, but we may be getting there.)

10. If you could change anything about the way you were raised, what would it be? (I've known Carter long enough to guess there's not really anything he'd have changed, but then one thing comes to mind. "You would have played more sports," I say with a confident smile. Apparently, other than one ill-fated season of T-ball in which he hated every minute, Carter didn't play organized sports as a kid. Where most kids would be glad their parents didn't force them to be involved in activities that didn't interest them, I've heard him say before that he wishes they hadn't let him quit. "Exactly," he says. "I didn't try out for

anything until high school and by then, I wasn't good enough to make the teams. But other than that, I'd say I had it pretty good.")

11. Take four minutes and tell your partner your life story in as much detail as possible. ("I don't think there's much here you could tell me that I don't already know," I say, smiling as I realize how well I really do know him. "I'd say that's a fair assessment," he says. "And at the moment, the story of my life is less interesting than the story of where my life is going.")

12. If you could wake up tomorrow having gained any one quality or ability, what would it be? (I think about this one for a minute. I've done pretty well at our little game/conversation so far, and I'd like to end with a win, but I'm coming up blank. "Okay," I say, shrugging. "I give up." "Well," he says, apparently also thinking it over. "I'd say I'd want whatever quality that would make you choose me." And in that moment, I realize how right he is. Whether we talk about them or not, the other men in my life have been with us this whole time. I'm truly on the verge of crying when he adds, "Or maybe X-ray vision.")

*

The rest of our hike through Cinque Terre is as beautiful and invigorating as the morning was. As the day goes on, more and more people join us on the trails, and I love hearing the other languages surrounding us as we make our way to through Corniglia to Manarola and finally to Riomaggiore. Each little town is beautiful in its own way and though I did truly love our hike, I am so thankful as we hop on the train and head back for Monterosso Al Mare at the end of our day. My legs feel like jelly and I could have fallen asleep on the bench at the station. I manage to stay awake not just on the ride back and on the walk to the car, but on the drive back over the mountain and a good portion of the way back to Trequanda. The scenery we couldn't see in the dark on our way here is beautiful and I'd feel bad sleeping the whole way there and back.

As soon as we get to the villa though, I know I'll be out as soon as I hit the pillow. The sleepy look on Carter's face tells me he feels the same, and we drag ourselves upstairs with some effort. Before we can fall onto the bed, I put my hand out to stop us.

"We're filthy," I say. "I don't want to ruin the bed."

"World's fastest shower?" says Carter.

"Deal." I strip and walk to the bathroom at the same time.

We shower together and it truly is a testament to how tired we both are that we don't immediately start kissing and such like we normally would in a joint shower situation. I'm thinking it might be the first time we won't actually have sex in the shower together when I open my eyes after washing my hair to see Carter looking at me with desire. Before I can ask if he's thinking what I'm thinking he closes the space between us and pulls me into him with a kiss. His hands slide over my slippery body, and his erection pushes between my legs.

I turn around to put my hands on the shower wall, go up onto my tiptoes, and moan as Carter enters me from behind. He's got one hand on my hip and the other coming around to caress my breast and every inch of my body is tingling with exhaustion and desire. My legs begin to shake as I try to keep myself at this angle and luckily Carter finishes quickly before my strength gives out. I laugh as we both clean ourselves up, realizing how silly it was to think we'd be able to avoid the obvious outcome of our naked, wet bodies, no matter how tired we are.

"Are we clean enough to get into bed yet?" he asks as I turn the water off.

"I do believe we are," I say, grabbing a towel.

And as we climb into bed and I fall asleep, I hear Carter humming part of a song that I will always associate with today.

"It's always better when we're together."

Chapter Twenty-Seven

www.flavorsofthemonth.bloggerific.com

Greetings from afar, friends! Sorry for the long wait for any updates from me, but I've been doing a fabulous job of relaxing and unplugging on my trip. I didn't want you all to think I'd forgotten you, so I decided to post a quick update to let you know I am alive and very, very well. Thank you all for respecting my privacy and still enjoying your Sinfully Good treats during this crazy time. Your support of our stores and me, personally, has meant the world to me. Until next time, ciao!

June 13

I send Sam an email after writing the blog post asking for an update on how things are going back home, then send a few emails and pictures to Kim and Meg while I'm online. I'm assuming all is well, or someone would have reached out to me by now. Maybe my absence was enough to get Gossip A to Z off my back and on to some other poor soul to torture. I shouldn't feel better about them targeting someone else, but in lieu of the site shutting down completely, "not me" feels like a decent alternative.

Carter and I are lounging at the villa today, making plans for our other adventures, including Rome. We've decided to book a place to stay in Rome so that we can spend two days there instead of one. I'm not sure even that will be enough, but we can get there early the day we leave if we want to see anything else and I do love it here away from the noise of the bigger cities. I'm just looking up the best tours and tips for us to try when I hear my phone ding, which is odd, because I don't have regular service here.

I reach for my phone and realize it's a WhatsApp notification, something I don't use often at home because normal texts work just fine.

> **Sam:** *Hi! I haven't wanted to bother you because Carter said not to, but since you reached out…*

> **Me:** *Oh no. What is it?*

> **Sam:** *Well, the protestors are still coming. There's not a ton of them and it's nothing I can't handle, but they're getting nastier, and I think it's because of the new article.*

I realize I'm holding my breath, so I exhale in a reverse gasp before bracing myself for what's to come. I turn back to the laptop and log on to the Gossip A to Z site, then let out an actual gasp as the page loads.

SINFULLY GOOD IN BED?

The headline is bad enough, but then I see a grainy video start to load below it and I want to throw up. It's really hard to see who the people are in the video, but it's a young, blonde girl and a dark-haired man clearly having sex. From the angle of the video, it's likely the girl has no idea she's being filmed, and her face is mostly obscured, but it would be pretty easy for people to assume it's me, especially with that headline.

Carter comes into the room and sees me staring at the screen in horror, asks something I can't hear, then sits beside me as I finish watching the video and read the text below.

> *Is this the kind of person you want to buy your kid's ice cream from? Cynthia Blake has always made herself and her stores out to be a family-friendly establishment, but would someone who appreciates family values ever allow themselves to be filmed having sex? And excuse us, but we're pretty sure she's never been married, and yet here she is — flaunting her sins for all the world to see. For all intensive purposes, she's basically advocating for young girls to sleep around and frankly, we're sick of it. Join us as we #boycottsin and send a message to Ms. Blake that we don't want her kind of business in our neighborhoods.*

Carter looks equal parts furious and concerned for me.

"We'll call the police," he says. "Or a lawyer? Who do we call to get them to take this down? They can't just put up some video and say it's you. This is libel. Or defamation. Or something. Are you okay?"

My lip is quivering and there are tears on my cheeks before I even realize I've started to cry. They are tears of rage, shame, and fear, but also maybe a little bit of relief to not be facing this alone.

"And how are they posting a video of two people having sex and claiming to have the moral high ground?" Carter says, continuing with his tirade. "That's pornography. And who knows where they got it. It looks like she doesn't even know she's being filmed."

"She doesn't," I say in a weak voice. "She's me."

*

It takes me a minute to find my courage, but I know I can't get through this alone, so it's time to see if Carter can handle me and the baggage I would bring to our lives.

"I was nineteen," I say. "I have never seen this video before, but I know it's me. It's me and the boy I was dating at the time. I can't believe he kept it all this time, but they must have paid him well for it. I don't even have his number anymore."

"Who was it?"

"I don't want to tell you that. You're a doctor. You could probably kill him and make it look like an accident."

Carter laughs, but it looks like the thought had crossed his mind.

"I, uh, understand if you want to head home," I say. "This isn't going to go away any time soon and I don't want you to get caught up in the chaos."

"Cyn, listen to me," he says, kneeling and taking my hands. "I'm not going anywhere. I still think we should call someone and see about getting this taken down though."

"Wouldn't that be admitting it's me? I think I should just ignore it."

"Ignore it?" His voice rises. "How do we ignore this?"

"Getting a reaction out of me is just what they want. They haven't been able to get pictures of me since we left, so they dug up dirt from my past. Any response from me just adds more fuel to the fire."

"If you say so," he says. "But when you're ready to fight, just know that I'm on your side. And I promise not to kill anyone."

Now it's my turn to laugh, but the sound feels unnatural coming from me. I try to put things in perspective. The tape is really grainy. It's not clear at all that it's me. People who want to hate me have probably already made up their minds, so this won't sway the masses. People who didn't care before either way might care a little more now, because, honestly, who can resist a sex tape? But maybe some people will hear about me and feel sympathetic. Or at least curious enough to come buy some ice cream? Even with the protests, our numbers have held steady. Maybe I can survive this.

The logical thoughts help, but I again feel a wave of shame and anger that I know I'm going to need to deal with. I want to unleash a bit of that on the jerk who filmed me without my knowledge, but if he was willing to sell a tape of me, I'm sure he'd love to sell an interview about me kicking him in the dick, which is what I'm picturing right now.

So, strike that, he's not worth it. Maybe I'll find out who's behind all these posts on Gossip A to Z when we get back and…and what? I can't yell at her or attack her, which also sounds cathartic. I don't know who she is, but she seems like someone who would sue if I even look at her wrong. And why am I assuming it's a woman? I mean, it has to be, with that kind of bitchy venom, but I should remember that it could be a man. Whoever it is, they suck.

I feel myself spiraling and realize I can't stay here today. I don't want this negative energy seeping into this beautiful place. I jump up off the couch, startling Carter in the process.

"Let's get out of here," I say. "Take me to whatever town is next on our list to explore."

"You got it, dude," he says, making me smile.

We're out of the door in five minutes and I feel better already, knowing that we're heading somewhere. I need to stretch my legs and find distractions. What better way to do that than to wander through another lovely Italian town? They're all so hilly in this area that it's pretty much been like hiking everywhere we've gone, so my achy legs post-Cinque Terre will just have to suck it up. The GPS is guiding us north and I let the views along the autostrada lull me into a daze. Is there no part of this country that's not stunningly beautiful?

As we exit the highway for a beautiful town up on a hill, I look down and see that our directions are taking us to a city I've heard of: Assisi.

"Why do I know that town?" I say.

"Because you know who Francis of Assisi is," says Carter. "Isn't he your favorite saint?"

I'm not sure if one should have a favorite saint, but I suppose if I do have one, it would be Francis. He helped the poor and downtrodden, from what I can remember. Not that I'd compare myself to the starving and miserable people he worked with when he was alive, but I'd say I'm feeling pretty low right now. Going to his hometown seems like a great option.

We find a place to park and begin walking the streets. It really is a lovely town, but the true beauty takes my breath away as we approach the big church we could see as we drove in. It is stark white and looks like it goes on forever. As we get closer, we see a statue of a man on horseback. His shoulders slump and his head hangs low. Is that Francis? He looks so sad.

We wander through the church and marvel in its opulence. Every little detail is pristine. Clearly, this man was beloved. We make our way down to the crypt where the bones of St. Francis lay. There is a bit of a line leading up to it and I notice each person in turn kneels before his sarcophagus before moving on. I am struck with sudden inspiration, so I join the line. Carter raises an eyebrow at me but joins me.

As my turn arrives, I also kneel and say this silent prayer:

"Saint Francis, I wonder if you could help heal the hearts of the people who are judging me? I feel like they must have some real anger and hurt in their lives if they feel the need to take it out on a stranger. If you can do that, I'd really appreciate it. I try to do good things in my life, and I'll definitely read more about you and do even more. I've probably been too selfish this year. Maybe always. Now I'm babbling. Long story short, if you could help those people feel better about their lives so they don't feel the need to bash me, that would be awesome. And if you're not too busy, I'd take some guidance on this huge, life-altering decision I'm supposed to make. Sorry to take so much of your time. Amen."

Carter kneels and spends a few seconds with our dude, Francis, too, before we move on to the rest of the church and the town. As we sit down for dinner at a restaurant that overlooks all of Assisi and the area surrounding it, I breathe a sigh of relief.

"What was that for?" asks Carter.

"That was me letting go of my anger," I say, truthfully. "I said before that I wasn't going to give them a reaction, and I mean that internally too. I won't let them ruin this trip or my life. That gives them too much power."

"That's very wise of you," he says. "But are you sure you can do that?"

I take stock of my feelings and wonder if I really can. I do feel calm right now, but small twinges of those negative emotions bubble just below the surface. It's not going to be easy.

"I'm not sure," I confess. "But I'm going to try."

Chapter Twenty-Eight

June 16

It must be easier to not dwell on negativity in Italy, because I really do manage to keep myself happy and distracted for the next several days. I can feel that latent anger bubbling up in weird ways, like when I almost cried because a gelato shop didn't have a flavor I wanted to try, but I really was craving chocolate. Still, for the most part, I am surprisingly serene for a woman who has just had a sex tape released without her consent.

Carter, to his credit, doesn't bring it up at all, and seems to be joining me in this lovely state of denial. We visit a few more wineries in the area, and each night enjoy the bottles we purchased locally after our passeggiata. We manage to even have sex without me freaking out and/or being reminded of what is now circulating the internet, for which I give the wine most of the credit.

Our overnight stay in Rome approaches and we both immerse ourselves in reading about all the places we want to see and things we'd like to do. I'm regretting that we only have one night there, but Carter keeps reminding me that we can always come back. It makes me smile every time he says it, as I imagine our future together. I can tell he feels the same way.

From our reading, and at the advice of the landlord who owns the bed and breakfast we've booked, we decide to take a train to Rome instead of driving. I love trains, hate the idea of having to find parking, and can tell we'll be able to navigate the city on foot anyway, so I'm in. And thus, we leave our little car at the train station nearest Trequanda and begin our Roman Holiday.

The train ride is uneventful until I get an idea.

"What's the train equivalent of the mile high club?" I ask Carter, with a devilish look on my face.

"Um, the two hundred kilometer per hour club?" he guesses, smiling at the look on my face. "Did you want to become a member?"

We're in a crowded train compartment, but there are bathrooms at both ends and I'm suddenly 100 percent sure that yes, I do want to join that club.

"You go first," I say with a quiet giggle. "I'll knock three times and then you let me in."

Carter needs no convincing and is soon out of his seat and down the aisle. I note that he goes into the bathroom on the left, give him a minute's head start, then make my way down to meet him. I congratulate myself on the foresight of wearing a dress today as I knock three times. The door opens, and I almost let out a laugh that would surely have given us away.

Carter is standing as far back in the tiny bathroom as he can so that he can let me in, pants and boxers around his ankles, full erection on display, and holding handfuls of paper towels, obviously meant for our use once we are done.

"You're so prepared!" I whisper before laughing again as I close the door behind me. There's barely enough room for him in here and I'm suddenly not sure this is going to work.

"Hop up on the sink," he says, clearly prepared for that thought as well. It's cramped, but I manage to sit and hike my skirt up, giving Carter enough room to put himself directly in front of me. He pulls my panties down and off, pops open the buttons on my dress to give himself a nice view of my lace-covered breasts, then presses himself inside me.

It's a bit uncomfortable as the faucet presses into my tailbone with each thrust, but as it was my idea, I decide not to say anything. The movement of the train and this angle, though, are hitting me in just the right places and it's the perfect combination of pleasure and pain. Seeing that I'm into it, Carter thrusts harder and harder, smiling as I welcome him in, wetter and wetter. He kisses my neck as I throw my head back and I bring back that devilish smile as I feel him finish, then pull out quickly to clean us both up.

"Welcome to the club," I say with a wink as I exit the bathroom and head back to our seats. I'm only few steps out of the door, though, when I realize I've forgotten my underwear. *Please let Carter pick those up*, I think, sitting back down awkwardly in my seat.

He comes out of the stall a moment later and I give him my best "Did you get my underwear off the floor?" face as he walks toward me. He nods and I wonder if I am actually telepathic.

"Lose something?" he says, handing me my balled-up panties.

"Why thank you, good sir," I say, taking them with a laugh. I put them in the front pocket of my bag and decide I can't get them back on in this seat without making a scene. I can't imagine our little tryst went completely unnoticed by other passengers, and I don't want to risk calling more attention to myself by getting up now, so I go commando for the rest of the trip.

"You're the only person I'd have sex in a train bathroom with," I say in a conspiratorial tone.

"Ditto," says Carter, wincing. "That was terribly uncomfortable. But super hot."

"Uncomfortable for you?" I scoff. "Which one of us had a faucet digging into her ass?"

"Ah, ouch. Let me know if you need that massaged later."

"After everything we've planned for such a short trip, I'm sure I'll be needing a full-body massage tonight."

"Deal," says Carter.

We spend the rest of the ride looking out of the window and as rural landscapes give way to the outskirts of the city, my heartbeat quickens with excitement. As much as I've loved relaxing and getting away from it all, there are just too many things I've always wanted to see nestled into the Eternal City. I am practically giddy.

We grab our bags and head for the exit, with me taking a quick stop in the restroom to re-panty myself. We've got another train to catch and a bit of a walk to the little apartment we're staying at just around the corner from The Vatican. After a quick map check that we're getting on the right route, we join a throng of tourists and locals, then keep an eye out for our stop. I'm wearing my backpack on my chest because that's what the guidebooks said to do and feel both silly and savvy. With how close we're pressed in this train car, it would be easy for someone to reach in and rob me.

Carter is smiling down at me as I cradle the bottom of the bag as if it's a baby.

"Laugh all you want," I say. "We'll see who's laughing when you lose your wallet."

"I was just imagining you pregnant," he says. "You're going to be adorable."

I flush and not because it's about a million degrees in here. Carter is thinking about our future in very real, very sweet ways. In all my relaxing, I've forgotten to really evaluate how I feel about him. About us. Do I even want to move forward with my plan after we get home?

On the one hand, I have no doubts about how I feel about Carter. I can see a path ahead for us and it really does seem like it leads to happily ever after. Haven't we proven that on this trip? We haven't fought or even argued, and it's been the best month of my life.

But is it that hard to live a peaceful existence in paradise? With no work, no chores, and no commitments each day, what do we even have to fight about? Maybe this wasn't the best idea for our month. How do I know this isn't just the vacation effect?

That's silly, I tell myself quickly. How unfair would it be to hold this trip against Carter after all the work he did in planning it? The effort he's made has to be in the pro column. I guess I can just list "not sure how we'd work on the real world" as a negative without pretending that Italy was a bad idea. We've usually gotten along back home as well, so I can't say I have no idea how things would go, but that wasn't actually a relationship, was it? It's easy to keep things smooth when there are no expectations of something more. Marriage is so much more.

"Where'd you go?" he says, interrupting my thoughts.

"Oh, uh, I was just trying to remember where we're supposed to be first today," I say, thankful for the distraction before I went into full panic mode.

"The Coliseum," he says. "We have our tickets and a thirty-minute window to use them so we can skip the queue out front."

"Queue?" I say. "You're *so* European now."

"Just trying to fit in 'round these parts," he says with a hint of Southern drawl.

"There's my all-American boy." I reach up to kiss his cheek.

*

As we step off the lift in the building that holds our home for the night, I feel a chuckle rise in my throat. What was advertised as a "spacious bed and breakfast in our lovely apartment" has got to be the most cramped space I've ever stayed in, if the rest of the apartments are anything to judge by. We've passed two open doors and they are comically small. I hold my breath as I knock on the door at number 11 and wait for our hosts.

"*Buongiorno!*" says a short, scruffy, but pleasant-enough looking Italian man. "Come in! Come in!"

We walk in and I relax a bit, noticing this is a corner unit and appears to be at least twice the size of the other apartments I saw. It's still pretty small, but if the other ones are normal for the area, I can forgive the "spacious" description.

Our host welcomes me with a hug and kiss on each cheek, then reaches for Carter to do the same.

"I am so happy you have come to stay with me," he says. "Here—let me show you to your room."

We follow him through the tiny living room and down the shortest hallway ever to a room with twin beds and a small balcony. It's small, but clean and cozy. The bed situation makes me a little sad, but I make a mental note that we can probably push them together.

"You need anything in Rome, you ask Guiseppe," he says, pointing to himself. "I live here all my life and I tell you all the things you need to know."

"Well, we're a bit hungry," I say.

"Of course, of course," he says. "You want to get food far away from the tourist places, okay? You have a map? I mark a few places for you."

We hand him the map we're planning to use, and I smile as he circles about twenty places, telling us who has the best of each type of food we could possibly want. He knows we're only here for a day, but I like that he's thorough. And who knows? Maybe we can eat a tiny bit at each location and have our own mini food tour of Rome.

"And for breakfast tomorrow," he says, "I show you."

He walks us into the galley kitchen and slides open a tiny box on the counter.

"Pastries are here," he says, pointing to some pre-packaged items, "and coffee is here."

With all the wonderful food options, I feel like eating these possibly stale, plastic-wrapped options is an insult to all of Italy, but he seems so eager for us to eat what he's provided that I make a mental note to throw a couple into our bag in case we get hungry on one of our tours tomorrow.

"Thank you so much, Giuseppe," says Carter magnanimously. "We're going to head out for the day, but maybe we'll see you later?"

"Yes, yes," he says, shooing us to the door. "Giuseppe is here if you need him. You try the food I circle, yes?"

"We'll do as many as we can," I promise, kissing him on both cheeks as we go to leave. He seems thrilled that I've returned this courtesy and I genuinely wish we were staying a bit longer so that we could hang out with Giuseppe even more.

As we walk out of the apartment building, I breathe in the city and reach for Carter's hand. Today is a good day, and we haven't even started exploring yet. My giddiness returns as we consult our map for the best way to get to the Coliseum. We find our way back to the underground system and take a quick ride to what looks like the best exit.

Walking out of the new station, it takes us a minute to get our bearings in the blinding, Roman sunlight.

"Which way is it?" I say, putting up a hand to shield my eyes from the sun as I squint to look around.

"Uh, Cyn?" says Carter. "Turn around."

A bus in the street behind me has moved on, and I turn around to see the Coliseum is right behind me. Huge, magnificent, and absolutely iconic, it towers over the cars passing by as if to say "I was here before you and I'll be here after you. Look upon me with reverence."

Or maybe it's an inanimate object and I'm projecting. Either way, it's pretty cool.

We pass by the idiots who were too stupid to buy tickets in advance and walk right through the entrance, as I pull out my headphones for us to share. I downloaded a guided tour onto my phone so we can explore at our leisure, which is just what we do.

From there, we make our way through the Forum and several other incredible sights. We find ourselves pretty hungry and right next to big tourist attractions, just like Giuseppe warned us about, but before I can consult our map to see if any of his recommendations are nearby, I see a familiar view. Golden Arches. And not ones adorning some ancient church. It's a McDonald's, sticking out like a sore thumb among all this beautiful architecture. I hear Carter scoff as he sees it too, then give him my biggest puppy-dog eyes.

"You don't seriously want to eat there," he says. "What about all of those places we wanted to try?"

"French fries," I say. "I want *french fries*."

"Damn," he says. "That actually does sound pretty good."

"Right? We can still eat the rest of our meals here at better restaurants. But right now, french fries sound amazing."

"Let's do it," he says. And we do. And they are salty, hot, and delicious.

"All the amazing food we've had on this trip and this is your favorite?" says an abashed Carter as I lick salt off my fingers.

"Absolutely not," I say. "But damn if that didn't hit the spot."

We both laugh and make our way back to the streets. I suggest that we ditch the map for a bit and just wander, confident that we'll stumble across something incredible if we just keep walking. I am proven right after a few blocks when we turn a corner and see the Pantheon directly ahead. We check that out, follow a few signs, and find ourselves in front of the Trevi Fountain.

"This," I say softly. "This I need to stare at for a minute."

"Stare away," he says. "It's pretty great."

There are so many things to see at this one space that I know my eyes can't possibly take it all in.

"We have to come back here at night," I say, inspired.

"I think that can be arranged," he says, taking my hand as we walk closer to toss our coins into the fountain.

We continue with our wandering, finding hidden treasures all throughout the city. Even the regular streets are just beautiful to stroll down.

Eventually, we are hungry again, and a quick check of our map shows that we are in between two of the Giuseppe-approved spots.

"What do you say we order one entrée at each?" I say.

"And one appetizer?" says Carter.

"Deal. And maybe a dessert at the second."

"Even better."

We do just that and decide it's a tie between the two places. We, however, are the winners, for being brilliant enough to think of going to both. Leaving the second spot takes us to a lovely church that sits at a high point in the city. I walk out to get a better look at it and realize it sits at the top of the Spanish Steps.

"How is everything here so iconic?" I say, marveling at what Rome has shown us so far.

"Iconic is in the eye of the beholder," says Carter. "You've been dreaming of these places since you were a girl."

Indeed, I have. And as we make our way back through the places we've already been to see how different they look at night, I feel like it's a completely new city. Somehow, everything is more magical at night, and my heart could just burst with joy at getting to see it all with someone I love.

I stop in my tracks at that thought as we come back to Trevi. Have I told Carter I love him on this trip? Or ever? I know I've thought it, but have I said it? Has he said it to me? I honestly can't remember. I know he's shown me, and I hope I've shown him, but I'm so confused now about what's been said aloud that I feel terrible. Has he been waiting all this time for me to say those words?

"What's wrong?" he says, realizing I'm a few steps behind.

"I just love…this city," I say, chickening out.

"It loves you too." He winks at me.

Okay, maybe we haven't said it to each other, but it certainly seems to be understood.

We stop at another Giuseppe recommendation, this time to share a bottle of wine at an outdoor table to people watch and rest our tired feet. The wine hits me hard and fast, and it seems to have the same effect on Carter.

"We've got a long day ahead of us," I say. "Should we make our way back to the apartment?"

"All ready for that massage?" he says back, slightly slurring.

I had forgotten about that, but now I've popped back up with a second wind.

"Guess that's a yes," he says, laughing as we down our last sips of wine and head for the exit.

We've walked so much that we're not too far from our apartment. We stop quickly to see St. Peter's and Castel San Angelo lit up at night (gorgeous), but then find ourselves back in the elevator that takes us to our room for the night. We use the key we picked up earlier and step in to find the place empty, which is just fine with me, as I'm now very much looking forward to my massage and everything that comes after.

We head into our room, and I pull my dress off over my head, leaving my bra and panties on for the time being. I lay down on the bed facedown and sigh as Carter quickly joins me, gently sitting on the back of my legs. He massages my shoulders, then my back, being very much the gentleman at first. He stands up to massage my butt and upper thighs and I moan as my muscles relax in relief. I really am sore, and this feels as therapeutic as it does sexy. After he's made his way down my whole body, he steps off the bed and I hear him undress. Soon, he's back on my legs, but this time he's naked and our massage quickly takes a turn.

He reaches up for my shoulders again, but this time he leans down to kiss me too, and his dick presses into my ass. My back rub becomes a chest massage as his hands reach around to cup and fondle my breasts and the sensation feels amazing. Everything is electric. I'm tired, tipsy, and ridiculously turned on. I can hear people passing under our window and I get a sudden bolt of inspiration.

"The balcony," I murmur.

"What?" he says, now massaging my belly and reaching one hand down toward my inner thighs.

"I want to have sex in Rome. Like outside—in Rome."

"Ahh," he says. "I suppose that can be arranged."

I stand up and walk my sexiest drunk walk toward the balcony and open the door. The space isn't big, but I don't want to be on it anyway. Just near it will be fine. I can see the moon and a bit of the city. This is what I wanted.

I turn around to see Carter, naked in the moonlight and I shiver. He's so fucking hot. And I feel pretty damn hot too, come to think of it. Unable to be away from my hotness, he comes closer and kisses me, hard. His tongue is amazing, and I want to feel it somewhere else.

"Go down on me," I whisper.

"As you wish," he says, dropping to his knees.

He pulls off my panties for the second time today and I spread my legs a bit to give him better access. Hungrily, he begins licking and sucking every inch of me, flicking his tongue around on my clit so hard that I wobble a bit where I stand.

"More," I say, and more he does, using fingers inside me and his tongue all around until I come and nearly scream. Now I really do feel like I might fall over, which I decide to play off by dropping to my knees and eagerly bringing his dick into my mouth. He is hard and perfect, and I can tell by his moans that he's loving this as much as I loved mine.

"Hang on," he says, pulling me back to standing.

"Something wrong?" I ask.

"The opposite. Keep doing that and I won't get to fuck you in Rome like you wanted."

I laugh, but with all the wine we've had and all the walking, I can't blame the guy. I turn back around so that I'm facing the balcony and take in the view again. I'm only wearing a bra now and Carter stands behind me, kissing my neck, reaching in to pinch my nipples and basically feel around however he can. I'm about to ask how he wants me when he moves my legs apart again and thrusts his throbbing erection into me.

I giggle for a second until I hear voices below us on the street again. I'm sure they can't see us, but the thought that they, or someone else, *could* see us makes my heart stop. I flash to a grainy video of nineteen-year-old me and feel like I might throw up. I didn't know I was being filmed then. I haven't known all year when people have been watching me. *What if someone is watching me right now?*

If Carter feels me go rigid, he doesn't mention it and he soon finishes. I try to pretend I didn't just have a panic attack while we were having sex, but as soon as I turn around, he can tell something is wrong.

"Did that hurt?" he says, looking concerned. "I wasn't sure if something happened right at the end there. You know you can always tell me to stop, right?"

I can't even answer, but I shake my head and try to get the word no to come out of my mouth, something to reassure him that it wasn't him. Instead, I start to cry and fall onto one of the beds in the fetal position.

"Whoa, whoa," he says. "What's wrong, baby?"

He's stroking my back and saying other encouraging things that should be helping me, but all I feel is every negative thought I've been squashing coming back to the surface and looking for a way to explode.

"I don't understand," he says, sweetly trying to get me to talk to him. But all I hear is the opening my rage has been waiting for.

"Of course, you don't understand," I say between sobs. "How could you? You're not the one with some sex tape going viral. No one filmed you without your knowledge. *No one is calling you a whore.*"

"Where did this come from?" he asks, looking completely blindsided. "Did someone see us on the balcony? That was your idea."

"Oh, like you tried to stop me," I say, knowing how irrational that must sound. "You're totally fine going along with it as long as you get off."

"We're both tired and drunk." His logic is impeccable. "Can we talk about this in the morning?"

Half of my brain shouts *yes*, but the other half will not be quieted so easily. I am hurting and freaked out; apparently, I cannot rest until he is too.

"I want to go home in the morning," I say, practically spitting out the words. "I don't want to be here anymore with you. I can't think straight here."

"What—what are you saying?" he says. He looks like I've slapped him. I wish that's what I'd done instead.

"I'm supposed to be using our month to figure out how I feel about us. But all I know is that I have no idea how we'd be back in the real world."

"What real world? This *is* the real world, Cyn. I was going to see if you wanted to go to Paris with me before we go home…"

"Paris?" I nearly scream. "You think this is the real world and so is Paris? These are my fantasies. These are the places I've always dreamed of going. I could have come here with a stranger and had the exact same trip."

I know I've gone too far when his eyes change from concern to anger.

"You think a stranger would have known all the places you've wanted to see?" he says, nearly whispering. I wish he'd yell. "You think one of your other guys would have taken five months to plan the trip of a lifetime, knowing all the while that you're out fucking someone else? Maybe you are a whore."

I've done it. I've pushed so hard with my toxic anger that I've brought it out of him too. I knew he couldn't be so okay with this whole thing as he's seemed all year. Maybe he doesn't actually mean what he's saying right now, but there's no going back.

"Maybe I am," I say. "And maybe whoever I end up with is just going to have to love me anyway. I thought you could have been the one, but—"

"But what, Cyn?" he says, tears streaming down his face. "What changed your mind all of a sudden? Because I *know* I'm the one. I can't believe what I just said. Please, please, let's talk again in the morning."

I roll over on my little bed, afraid to face him with everything between us still lingering in the air.

"Morning," I say. "Sure, we'll talk in the morning."

Chapter Twenty-Nine

June 12

I wake the next day with Italian sunlight streaming across the room and onto my puffy face. My rage tears must have been leaking as I slept. I feel about a hundred years old. I roll over to see if Carter is still sleeping. His bed is empty. I throw some clothes on and go out to see where he might be.

The kitchen is empty, but Giuseppe sits at his desk in the living room. I'm about to turn to see if Carter is in the bathroom, when I hear our host clear his throat.

"Ah, good morning, signora," he says awkwardly. "Your friend, he ask me to give you this."

He hands me a few folded pieces of paper with my name scrawled along the top.

Cynthia,

You need to figure out what you want back in the "real world," and I still need to clear my head out here in fantasyland. I changed your ticket to this morning. I checked and your passport is in your backpack. I'll bring the rest of your stuff back when I fly home next week. I'm sorry for what I said last night, but I don't want to spend the rest of this trip fighting with you.

See you back in the States,

Carter

I check the pages underneath to find my boarding pass and record of the flight changes he had to make, which I'm sure I'll need in case the airline questions my itinerary. My eyes are blurry from fresh tears, and I hate that I'm crying in front of a stranger, but something about the tickets looks weird to me. I accept the tissue Giuseppe hands me and use it to clear my vision as best I can.

Something along the top of my ticket has been scratched out. Carter left the confirmation numbers, but apparently, we weren't heading back to Arizona straight from Rome. What did he say last night about going somewhere else?

I hold the paper up to the light and can see through the pen markings that we were supposed to connect through Charles de Gaulle airport before we went home. Then I see the dates. It wasn't just a stopover. He booked us two days in Paris.

My mind flashes back to a text I sent last month. A text about where I want to be proposed to someday.

Carter was taking me to Paris.

Carter was going to propose.

Santa merda del cazzo.

Acknowledgements

It takes a village to get a book into the world. Heck, if you're me, it takes a village to do damn near anything. I am abundantly blessed to have the village I do and especially want to thank one group in particular with this book. To my BNI family, my Shark brothers and sisters, thank you for welcoming me into your community and constantly pushing me to be a better version of myself. You make me confident to introduce myself as a writer and inspire me each week.

Experiencing a dream come true without my dad here to witness it has been bittersweet to say the least, but how lucky I am to have a mom and sister who carry him with me as I do to cheer me on a little extra in his absence. Mom, Nikki—only the women who were loved by Paul McLean can know what we know. Thank you for reflecting him and all the best moments of our family back to me always.

Thank you also to my husband, Mark, for supporting my crazy notions like writing these books in the first place and being brave enough to just smile and nod as readers work out which of the men you are in this series. Thank you for being my first, my last, my everything. I like you and I love you.

Thank you to my mother-in-law, Candy, for handing me a romance novel years ago and sparking my realization that I could write like this for a living. And then thank you for being one of my first readers no matter how uncomfortable some of the scenes made you. I must also thank you for showing me this beautiful world so I could write about it.

Brittany and Nicci—my first readers and first fans! It's hard to believe I've been bugging you guys about these books for nine years now, but I truly wouldn't have finished nor published them without you. Thank you for 20+ years of friendship and here's to 20+ more.

Thank you to my team at NineStar, especially Elizabeth and Rae. Your belief in me as a writer and efforts to get my stories into the world will rank among the best things a human has ever done for me.

To my kids, who I once again hope will not read these books for a very long time, thank you for being the joy of my life. Where you lead, I will follow.

And to the rest of my family and friends who have rooted for me for years, months, or even the newest readers who are just now finding me, thank you for reading this and giving me purpose.

About Penny McLean

Penny McLean is a careerwoman by day, writer by night, mother at all times to three incredible children, and wife to a loving husband. Born in San Diego, California, she now hails from Gilbert, Arizona where she especially enjoys giving back to her community by volunteering at schools and libraries, with Girl Scouts, and for any causes that benefit marginalized communities, especially LGBTQIA+ youth. She began her career as a writer at the age of 17 when she was hired to cover movies, arts, and features for a youth-oriented page in the *Arizona Republic*. With twenty years of writing experience for magazines, newspapers, social media, and more, she is thrilled to have her first novel out in the world.

Website

www.nerdygirlapproved.com

OTHER NSP BOOKS BY THIS AUTHOR

Flavors of the Month Series

The Plan

Coming Soon from Penny McLean

The Proposal

Flavors of the Month, Book Three

Apparently, I was so drunk on the flight home, they almost didn't let me board. I don't remember this, but the man I'm sitting across from at dinner certainly does.

"And then," continues the man, "I saw that you were about to pass out, so I pulled you up into my arms and told the flight attendant you were my girlfriend and just a really nervous flyer. Luckily, we were seated next to each other, so she totally bought it. I pretty much dragged you down the jetway."

He laughs and looks at me knowingly over this shared memory that only he remembers. I am mortified, but he could not be nicer about the whole thing.

"And I slept on your shoulder the whole way here?" I ask.

"You were in and out," he says. "We talked a bit, but I guess nothing stuck?"

"Sorry, no." I take a moment to really look at him as he gives his order to our waiter. We got off the plane together and he suggested that I eat something, so we're sitting at a restaurant in Terminal 4 of Sky

Harbor Airport. I told him in no uncertain terms it's my treat, which seems like the least I can do now I know I only made it home because of his help.

He is built like a linebacker, which eases my worry about him basically carrying me onto the plane. He looks like someone who would have played football at one of those big schools in the Midwest. In fact, his shirt sleeves can barely contain his biceps. And his face reminds me of someone. Who is that wrestler who is now an actor? Damn. That's going to bug me.

"What did we talk about?" I say after ordering a burger and fries. I'm back in the USA and might as well eat like it.

"I told you I'm a fireman and you said you've always wanted to sleep with one of us," he says, causing me to nearly spit my sip of water on him.

"I did not," I say.

"You did." He laughs so hard he looks like he might cry. "Not something I haven't heard before, but usually not so early in a conversation."

"I am so sorry. I am jet-lagged and I was obviously really drunk and—"

"Really, it's fine. I could tell you'd been crying and you said something about coming from Italy, so I knew you were tired and having a tough time. And it's never a bad day when a beautiful woman says she'd like to sleep with me."

Connect with NineStar Press

WWW.NINESTARPRESS.COM

WWW.FACEBOOK.COM/NINESTARPRESS

WWW.FACEBOOK.COM/GROUPS/NINESTARNICHE

WWW.TWITTER.COM/NINESTARPRESS

WWW.INSTAGRAM.COM/NINESTARPRESS